Praise for *T*
The first Book in the *Our America* Series

When I first informed my 10 year old that I had a new book for her to read for school, she let out a sigh combined with a look like, "Oh, great!...That means something I won't enjoy." Little did she know that an exciting journey awaited her. She began reading and within the first chapter informed me that she already loved the book! She was taken away into a world of adventure seeking to discover a mystery.... Thank you, Susan Kilbride, for the fantastic opportunity to teach my children about their rich heritage and to keep them excited about learning more.

By Tammy Wollner
Author of *Keeping His Way Pure*

My 11 year old son, who has no desire to learn from a textbook about the pilgrims and memorize boring dates, eagerly read The Pilgrim Adventure. *A living book,* The Pilgrim Adventure *combines real facts with some fiction to make the subject more appealing.*

Tina from Newbeehomeschooler.com

I finally found time to sit down to read Our America....The Pilgrim Adventure, *by Susan Kilbride, and ended up reading it in two sittings, it flows so smoothly. What a perfect way to share history with children — and adults! I learned a few things here, too!*

Gail Nagasako
Author of *Homeschooling Why and How*

The historical appeal makes this book a perfect addition to your studies on American history. My children were able to retain so much more information in this format than a simple text. I am never a fan of entertainment over education, but this book does not fall into that. The book is fun and contains fantasy, yet the historical accuracy and overall feel of the story give it the perfect blend of entertainment and education.

Richele McFarlin from Families.com

Susan knows what homeschoolers are looking for and delivers that in her books.

Heidi Johnson from Homeschool-how-to.com

I love how Finn and Ginny become a part of the story and participate in the unfolding of the pilgrims' experiences when they arrive at Plymouth. I found myself, while reading it, forgetting that it was also educational! An especially nice fact about this book is that the author obviously knows her facts on the pilgrims and Mayflower.....She very effectively brings these people to life in an interesting way for the reader.

Joy from Homeschoolliterature.com

Susan Kilbride, homeschool mother and author, has done it again! Our America....The Pilgrim Adventure *is Susan's first book in her new* Our America *series, and it is a wonderful way to involve kids of all ages in learning about early America....The storyline involves homeschooled twins, Finn and Ginny, in a search for their missing parents. This fantastic search lands the twins aboard the Mayflower and eventually the new land. Mystery and adventure keep your attention while historical facts are seamlessly woven into the story.*

Jackie from Quaint Scribbles

Our America....
The King Philip's War Adventure

For some free activity ideas to accompany this
book, visit the author's website at
http://funtasticunitstudies.com/

Other Books by Susan Kilbride

Science Unit Studies for Homeschoolers and Teachers

The *Our America* Series

The Pilgrim Adventure
The King Philip's War Adventure

The *How to Teaching Guides*
Available as Kindle eBooks

How to Teach a Newspaper Class
for Middle and High School Grades

Our America....

The King Philip's War Adventure

Susan Kilbride

Funtastic Unit Studies
USA

http://funtasticunitstudies.com/

Our America....
The King Philip's War Adventure

Copyright © 2012 by Susan Kilbride

The front and back cover art is adapted from art found in the books *Soldiers in King Philip's War* by George Madison Bodge, 1906, and *The History of the Indian Wars in New England*, Vol. 1, by Rev. William Hubbard, 1865 edition.

Distributors and retailers can purchase this book directly from the publisher at:
www.createspace.com/info/createspacedirect

ISBN-13: 978-1477537220

ISBN-10: 1477537228

Acknowledgements

First, I would like to thank my family and friends for all of their kind words and encouragement. I could never have done this without you! I would also like to thank the parents and children who read the first book in this series, *The Pilgrim Adventure,* and told me that they could hardly wait for the next book to come out. You pushed me to write it much sooner than I had planned!

I would also like to thank Ellen Barski, who graciously offered to help me with editing. Her great advice, corrections, and encouragement helped make this book better than I had imagined it could be. Any grammar mistakes you might find in this book are probably ones I made after she looked over the book. Nancy Bestul also gave me some excellent writing advice.

Finally, I would like to thank everyone who has helped me with my genealogical studies through the years. I have found that genealogists are some of the nicest researchers around. They are always willing to help a stranger with a genealogical puzzle. Since genealogy sparked my interest in history, these books may never have been written without the kindness of strangers.

Susan Kilbride

A Note to Parents

King Philip's War was a horrible war in terms of the atrocities that each side inflicted on the other. I have not gone into them in detail in this book because that would not be appropriate for children. However, the historical events in this book really happened, and there are deaths that occur in the story that might be upsetting for very young readers. That is why I have suggested that this book and the others in the *Our America* series be for children ages 10 and up. I know that there are some young fans of *The Pilgrim Adventure* who are under age 10, so I suggest that their parents might want to read *The King Philip's War Adventure* first and decide if they think that their children under 10 can handle it. Or perhaps parents might edit out parts of the book while reading it aloud to younger children.

I hope you all enjoy reading this book as much as I have enjoyed writing it!

Susan Kilbride

Conscience....then the War is over, for that was what they were searching for, it being much wanting.

Captain Benjamin Church's comments after capturing a Native American man named Conscience

1

A New Adventure

That's it!" exclaimed Finn as he slammed down the book he'd been reading. "I've had it. I can't take this anymore!"

"What are you complaining about now?" asked Ginny wearily. Lately it seemed as if Finn was getting upset over just about everything.

"I'm tired of sitting around and doing nothing about finding Mom and Dad. I want to go back in time again to look for them."

Ginny quickly sat up. "I thought we'd agreed that it was too dangerous. You were the one who said that I'd almost died in the past, and that we shouldn't go again."

"I know that's what I said," grumbled Finn, "but I've been thinking about Mom and Dad trapped back in time, and it's just as dangerous for them. If we don't go back and find them, we may never see them again, and I'd always feel that it was my fault for not trying."

Ginny thought about how their parents had been trapped in the past by accidentally activating the remote control to her Uncle Peter's time machine. Then, she and Finn had used it to go looking for them and had found themselves on the Mayflower.*

"Well, you were the one who decided that we shouldn't go back," she said.

Finn looked over at her. "It's just that I thought that you were going to die back in time. What good is it saving Mom and Dad if I lose you?"

"Well, don't I have a say in this?" demanded Ginny. "They're my parents, too. I want to go look for them again!"

Finn grinned at her. "Don't get so upset. So do I! That's why I've been so grumpy lately. I couldn't make up my mind about what to do."

"Well, just because you're grumpy about something doesn't mean you should take it out on the people around you," lectured Ginny.

Then she thought for a moment. "You know, Uncle Peter and Aunt Martha are going to that party tomorrow night. Why don't we go then? The last time we went back to the past we were only gone from the present for about five

---

*The Pilgrim Adventure

minutes, so we should have plenty of time while they're at the party."

"Sounds good to me," said Finn. The twins looked at each other in relief. They were finally going to try to find their parents again.

* * * *

The next evening the twins waved goodbye to their aunt and uncle and waited until the last sounds of the car had faded away. It was time to leave for their next adventure into the past. Ginny gave a little shiver.

Finn looked at her in concern. "Are you okay?

"Yes, I'm fine. I don't know what came over me. Maybe a goose walked over my grave or something," she laughed.

They walked into the living room and sat on the couch with the time-traveling remote control in front of them. Finn looked at Ginny.

"Are you sure you're ready to do this again? Remember how hard things were back in the old days. Last time we were there for over a year, but there's no way of knowing how long we'll be gone this time."

"I'm ready," said Ginny confidently. "I want to find Mom and Dad." She gave a quick grin. "At least this time we know better than to pack anything, since it won't get transported with us."

Finn grinned back. "Well, I'm glad that we don't have to worry about our clothing. I have no idea how our clothes change into the proper ones for the time period when we time travel, but I'm sure glad they do. Can you imagine what the people in the past would think if we suddenly appeared wearing modern-day clothes?"

Ginny laughed. "They'd probably throw us in prison or something!"

Their grins faded and the twins solemnly looked at each other. They knew that once they started the time machine, anything could happen. There was no going back. Finn picked up the time-remote, and Ginny grabbed on to his arm. Finn put his finger on the button that would take them back in time.

At that same moment, the twins' Labrador, Corky, came bounding into the room, wanting to play.

"Wait, Finn!" yelled Ginny as Corky leaped up on her. She started to fall over—just as Finn pressed the button on the time-remote.

Finn could feel that he and Ginny were being pulled back in time. The world started spinning and his stomach started churning. Then, he felt Ginny's grip on his arm loosen. He frantically grabbed for her, but it was too late. They had become separated back in time.

2

A New Relative

Finn landed on his back and lay there trying to catch his breath as he waited for the dizziness caused by the time machine to subside. When the world stopped spinning, the first thing he noticed was that he felt wet and cold. He took a quick look around. He was in a snowy wilderness with no buildings in sight. About twenty feet away, a column of men were trudging along carrying muskets and looking grim. Ginny was nowhere to be seen. He closed his eyes in despair. His worst nightmare had happened. He'd lost not only his parents, but his sister, too.

"Finn, is that you? Whatever are you doing out here?"

Finn looked up in confusion. A young man leaned over him.

"Don't you recognize me? I'm your Uncle Ben—Ben Webster. You may not remember me. You were pretty young the last time I saw you." Uncle Ben reached down and helped Finn to his feet. "But how did you end up out here in the middle of nowhere?"

Finn quickly remembered that the time machine always sent them back to places where their ancestors lived, so this must be one of his ancestors. But how could he answer the question when he didn't even know where he was? Then he thought of something.

"I'm looking for my sister."

The man's jaw dropped. "You've lost Ginny? Was she captured by Indians?"

Now it was Finn's turn to look shocked. "I...I don't know," he stammered. "She was with me one minute, and the next minute she was gone. I have to find her!" he exclaimed.

Uncle Ben looked worriedly at Finn. "Well, you'd better come with me for now. We can't leave you out here by yourself. I don't know what we're going to do with you once the fighting starts. I'll have to ask Lieutenant Swain where you can go."

"Fighting? What fighting?" asked Finn.

Uncle Ben looked at him curiously. "What do you think we're doing way out here with our muskets? We're going to fight the Indians, of course. Word has it that a large group of Narragansetts have built a fort in a swamp not far from here, and we're going to root them out."

Finn just nodded. What was going on? When he'd left the Pilgrims in 1621, they were starting to make friends with their Indian neighbors. Something had obviously gone horribly wrong. But what had happened? He decided to keep quiet until he could figure out what was going on here. In the meantime, he'd keep his eyes open for either Ginny or his parents.

As he trudged alongside his new-found uncle, Finn suddenly remembered the time-remote. He had quickly slipped it into his drawstring pocket when he first landed in the snow. Now he pulled it out and looked at the number on the screen; 148. That was how many days he had before the machine sent him home to the future.

That was how long he had to find Ginny before she would be trapped back in time. Just like their parents.

3

The Battle Begins

They reached the edge of the swamp that afternoon. Uncle Ben found Lieutenant Swain and explained that Finn was a young relative whom he'd found lost in the woods. The lieutenant told Uncle Ben to take Finn where General Winslow was directing his troops, since he would be safer there.

"General Winslow?" Finn asked when Uncle Ben told him where to go. "Is he any relation to Edward Winslow?"

"I'd say!" Uncle Ben laughed. "The general is Edward Winslow's son. I thought everyone knew that."

As Finn walked over to General Winslow, he decided that it probably wasn't a good idea to mention that he'd met the general's father. He and Ginny had met him the last time they had traveled to the past, during the time of the Pilgrims. Edward Winslow had felt it very important to develop good relations with his Indian neighbors, so Finn wondered what his son was doing leading a group of men against the Narragansetts. He didn't like this situation he'd found himself in at all.

Finn had barely reached the general's headquarters when shots rang out from the swamp. The fighting had begun, and it was not very far away. Finn could hear shots, screaming, and the sounds of chaos.

Finn sat on a nearby stump and wondered what he and Ginny had gotten themselves into. What if Ginny had been captured by the Indians? What if she was caught in the middle of the battle? It was possible that she had landed back in time not far from him, so she could be right in the middle of the fighting. The shouts and screams grew louder as more and more men rushed into the battle.

Nearby, the general and two men were peering down at a map. Benjamin Church, one of General Winslow's aides, paced up and down next to them, frustrated at being left out of the action. He stopped and stared into the swamp as the noise from the battle intensified. He quickly turned to the general.

"Sir, can I take some men and join the battle?"

The general nodded thoughtfully. "It sounds as if they could use some help in there, and I don't need you here for the moment. If you can find some men to go with you, you have my permission to join the fight."

Finn watched as Church and the thirty men headed into the swamp. The noise from the swamp was getting louder and more intense. Finn sat and worried. Then, after what seemed like forever, Finn saw two men come stumbling out of the trees, one leaning on the other. He quickly ran to help them. The injured man was Benjamin Church. His leg was covered in blood and his face was wracked with pain. Finn grabbed one of his arms and helped haul him over to General Winslow.

Church took some deep breaths, straightened himself up, and said, "General, the men are burning the wigwams inside the fort, and I ask you to reconsider. The fort is a good strong one and easy to defend. The wigwams are musket-proof, since they are lined with baskets of grain. We could use them to shelter the wounded from the cold tonight, especially since it will be dark soon. Plus, our army needs the provisions that are inside them."

The general considered. "That sounds like good thinking, Church. I will ride in immediately and bring the rest of the army."

Finn jumped up to follow the men into the swamp. Suddenly, a man stepped up and laid his hand on General Winslow's horse.

The general drew back. "Captain Moseley, what's the meaning of this?"

"Sir, you can't go in there. It's not safe! Your life is worth a hundred of theirs. You should not expose yourself!"

"But Master Church says that the fort has been taken and that it would be a practical place for us to shelter," answered the general.

"No, sir. Church lies! It's not safe, and if you take another step, I'll shoot your horse right out from under you!"

At that moment an army doctor spoke up. "We can't keep the wounded in there tonight. If we do, by morning they will be so stiff that we won't be able to move them. We must get them out of here tonight."

The general looked uncertainly between the three men, and then said to Captain Moseley, "Well, go ahead then and burn the wigwams. If we aren't going to use them, we can't leave them or the fort here for the Indians to come back to."

Finn could stand it no more. He had to find out what was happening in the swamp. Ginny might be caught in the midst of it. He broke away from the men and ran toward the fort.

"Wait, boy, come back here," yelled Captain Moseley, but Finn kept running. Running into a nightmare.

4

A World Gone Mad

Finn ran into the swamp until he saw the fort. It was a palisade of tall logs lined up next to each other and lined by a thick wall of brush and clay. Off to one side was a group of Indian prisoners under guard. Finn rushed over the log leading into the main entrance and stopped in horror.

Inside the fort were hundreds of wigwams, many of them on fire. People trapped inside them were screaming for help. Why hadn't Church mentioned that there were people still in the burning wigwams?

Finn rushed up to one of them and poked his head through the entryway. Inside two young faces looked up at him in fear. He reached in to get the children and take them to safety, but they scrambled away from him, eyes wide with terror.

"Don't be scared, I won't hurt you," Finn pleaded, but they just shied away from him.

The wigwam was filling with smoke and time was running out, so he just reached in and grabbed them, one under each arm, and hauled them kicking and screaming from the wigwam. He looked wildly around for a safe place to take them. Then he remembered the Indian prisoners under guard at the entrance to the fort. He ran with the children back over the log entrance and thrust them at the first Indian woman he saw. Then he rushed back into the fort to try to rescue more people.

On his way back in, he saw a soldier standing in the middle of the surrounding chaos. Finn ran up to him.

"Quick, help me try and get some of these people out of the wigwams!"

The man scowled. "After what the Indians have done to us, you expect me to help them now?" He spat on the ground and stomped away.

A young soldier who had heard the whole exchange looked sympathetically at Finn and said, "He's wrong, you know, or at least partially wrong. The Narragansetts have mostly been trying to stay out of the fighting, though I've heard that some of their young men have joined the Pokanoket attacks. And of course, some of the wounded Pokanokets who are here did participate in the attacks on our towns. But even so, it's not right to burn the wounded in their beds, or to kill their women and children, no matter what they've done to us. I'll help you."

Together Finn and the young soldier searched the wigwams and pulled people out, mostly the very young, old, or wounded—people who weren't able to get out by themselves. The smoke was thick and it was getting harder and harder to breathe.

"This must be what hell is like," reflected Finn. There were dead men lying everywhere, both Indian and English. As he walked by one body, he thought, *"Why does that man look familiar? I don't know anyone here."* He looked closer. Uncle Ben! He ran back, bent down to examine him, and gave a start of surprise—Uncle Ben was still alive! Finn motioned to the helpful soldier, whose name he had discovered was John, and together they carried Uncle Ben outside the fort to where the doctor was caring for the wounded.

"Can you help him, doctor? Will he be all right?" Finn asked worriedly. Then he remembered that Uncle Ben was his ancestor. If Uncle Ben died here on this battlefield without having any children, would Finn and Ginny suddenly disappear?

"It looks as though he was shot in the leg and then hit his head when he fell," said the doctor. "I'll dig out the musket ball, but you'll have to rig up some way to carry him the sixteen miles back to the garrison. We'll be leaving in about half an hour, so you'll have to hurry if you want him to live."

Finn stared at him. "Carry him?"

"Unless you can get him awake and walking by then," the doctor said dryly. "A blizzard is almost upon us, and we need to get moving."

Frantically Finn wondered how he could carry Uncle Ben all the way to the garrison. Then he remembered the survival course he had taken the year before.

"I know! We can make a travois!" Finn quickly turned to John, who was standing nearby. "Do you have a hatchet that I can borrow?"

"Sure do," the young man replied. "I also know where there is some rope we can use."

"Great! I think we can do this if we hurry," said Finn.

While John went off for the rope, Finn used the hatchet to cut down two saplings about ten feet long. He laid them down in a triangular shape, but then he stopped short.

"The travois in the survival course was pretty hard to move with a heavy load, and we've got to carry Uncle Ben sixteen miles. Maybe I can change the design a bit to make it more like a ladder. That way we can use it as either a travois or a stretcher. Then we can switch off how we use it when we get tired."

He laid the saplings out parallel to each other and lashed more sticks across the two saplings so that it looked a bit like a ladder. He took some of the rope and wove it between the sticks, and then placed a blanket he had borrowed from the doctor on top of the whole thing. By the time he was finished, it was almost time to go.

The doctor had dug the musket ball from Uncle Ben's leg and bandaged the wound. Finn and John laid him on the travois and covered him with a second blanket. Finn stepped into the front section of the travois, picked it up, and started the long sixteen-mile march in the dark and snow to the garrison. As he walked away, the light from the burning fort lit up the sky for miles around.

It was a miserable night. Finn and John took turns either hauling the travois or carrying it like a stretcher. By the end of the night they were so exhausted they could barely speak. Plus, Finn was in shock from all of the horrors that he had witnessed. His thoughts whirled.

"Has the whole world gone crazy? Why are the English colonists and Indians killing each other? What happened since the last time he was here?" But always, his thoughts ended with one big question:

"Where is Ginny?"

5

Lancaster

"Ginny, are you hurt?"

Ginny stared up at the young man who was looking worriedly down at her. She had no idea where she was, but she figured that the man above her must be one of her ancestors.

"No, thank you, I'm fine," she said quickly as the young man helped her stand up. She glanced around and saw that they were in front of a small one-story building, nestled in the snow. Finn was nowhere to be seen.

The young man smiled at her and said, "You can go with your Aunt Hannah into the meeting house. I'll follow you in shortly."

That was when Ginny noticed the young woman next to her, whom she figured must be married to the young man.

The woman smiled and said to Ginny, "Are you ready to go in now? You didn't hurt yourself, did you?"

"No, I'm really fine," Ginny said stoutly, though inside she was panicking. Where was Finn?

Ginny followed her new Aunt Hannah, who was carrying a baby and holding the hand of a little girl who looked about two years old, into the one-room meeting house. Ginny knew from her last experience in the past that a meeting house was a type of church. As her eyes adjusted to the dim light inside, she saw that the men were sitting on one side of the room and the women on the other.

She settled herself on to one of the most uncomfortable pews she'd ever sat on, and chewed her lip in worry. Since Corky had knocked her away from Finn, they must have gotten separated in the past. She quietly searched herself, but she didn't have the time machine remote, which meant that Finn must have it. She had no idea how many days they would be here in the past, but if she didn't find Finn and the time-remote before their time was up, she might get stuck in the past just like their parents. She needed to find Finn, but girls back in the past just didn't go off traveling by themselves. Plus, what if Finn was looking for her, and she was looking for him, and they kept missing each other?

After some thought, Ginny decided that it would be best if she stayed put to make it easier for Finn to find her. He'd been in the past before, so he knew how hard it was for girls to travel. But what year was it anyway? She looked down at her clothes. When the time machine sent them back into the past, it changed their clothes into the proper ones for the time period they were in. She seemed to be wearing similar clothes to what she had worn when living with the Pilgrims: a shift covered with a skirt and a vest-like bodice, with a drawstring bag under her skirt for a pocket. That must mean that she was back in colonial times again. She definitely was not going to be able to travel around alone. Finn was just going to have to find her.

* * * *

A few hours later, when the church service was over, Ginny followed Aunt Hannah and Uncle Jonathan to their home. The meeting house had not been heated, and Ginny was freezing, so it was nice to sit in the main room of their house in front of a cozy fire. She was unhappy though, because most of the town had been at the church service, and she hadn't seen her lost parents anywhere. Now, both she and her parents were lost in time. She felt so helpless, just having to sit and wait for Finn to find her. Surely there was something she could do to help him.

Then she had an idea.

"Uncle Jonathan, do you know anyone in other towns that you could write to? Maybe they have heard word of my brother."

Jonathan rubbed his chin thoughtfully. "What a good idea, Ginny. I can think of a few people I could write. Though it will be hard to get anyone to deliver letters with the war going on."

"War?" Ginny thought. *"What war would this be? I can't ask outright, or they won't understand why I don't know already."*

"How did this war start?" she asked.

"Oh no, here we go again!" sighed Hannah. "My Jonathan has very definite ideas about the war!"

Jonathan smiled. "Well, Ginny, it's a long story, but I think that basically it comes down to greed. The greed of the colonists for the land that they could buy from the Indians, and the greed of the Indians for the goods that they could receive from the colonists, without either party taking into consideration how the Indians would survive without their land. We all got too greedy, and now we are all paying the price."

He sighed and then went on.

"You see, back in England, it is very crowded compared to here. When the English settlers first came here to New England, they were amazed at how much empty land there was. And much of it was truly empty. Many Indians who had lived on it had died from various illnesses they had caught from the Europeans who had been trading with them. That's what happens when two groups of people meet for the first time. They pass their illnesses to each other."

Ginny nodded. She had learned this from her time with the Pilgrims.

Uncle Jonathan continued, "So more settlers started coming, and they started purchasing more and more land from the Indians, and the Indian leaders kept selling more and more of their land to the settlers. It's been over fifty years since the Pilgrims came to Plymouth, and we thought that things were going along pretty well with our Indian neighbors. Life has been peaceful for a while now, but I guess that some of the Indians have been getting angry about how much of their land we now own and about how much influence we have in the area, and they decided that they want us out of here. The problem is that this is now our home too, and we have no place to go back to. I've lived here most of my life. My family moved here when I was a baby, and this is the only home that I've ever known. There is no place for me in England."

"They've decided to murder us all," said Aunt Hannah angrily. "They killed eight people in our town in August, including two innocent children, and they've also attacked Middleborough, Dartmouth, Mendon, Brookfield, Deerfield, Hadley, Northfield, and Springfield."

"So you see Ginny, it's going to be hard to send out letters about your brother right now, though I will try," said Uncle Jonathan. "The militia passes through from time to time, so I can send some letters on with them."

"Thank you," said Ginny quietly. What had she gotten herself into? And how was she ever going to find Finn with a war going on?

6

Safety

After what felt like the longest night of his life, Finn trudged into the garrison at Wickford, carrying one end of the homemade travois-stretcher that held his Uncle Ben. He nodded gratefully to John for all of his help, as members of the garrison rushed out to relieve them of their load. Then they both stumbled off for some much-needed rest. Later they found out that the battle they had just left was being called "The Great Swamp Fight."

The following afternoon, after sleeping for twelve hours straight, Finn went searching for Uncle Ben to see if he had survived the journey. He'd heard that twenty-two of the wounded men had died along the way.

As he searched for Uncle Ben, he heard a lot of angry muttering about officers who forced wounded men to walk sixteen miles in a blizzard.

"I heard that Benjamin Church tried to convince General Winslow to stay in the fort," one man said as Finn walked by.

"Perhaps the general should have listened to him," another man answered.

Finn was having the same thoughts as he heard more and more horror stories of men dropping dead in their tracks or freezing their toes off. The general's group had even gotten lost and wandered around in the dark for hours before they got back on track again.

Finally he found Uncle Ben in a room full of wounded men. He was sitting up in bed, though he still looked weak and in pain. His eyes lit up when he saw Finn.

"There you are, young Finn! Am I glad to see you!" he exclaimed. "I hear that I have you to thank for saving my life and hauling me away from that inferno."

Finn smiled. "I'm just glad that you made it, sir."

He glanced over at the bed next to his uncle and was surprised to see Benjamin Church, who was also sitting up.

"Master Church here was just telling me an interesting story about King Philip, the Indian sachem who started this war," said Uncle Ben.

Master Church cleared his throat. "Yes, as I was saying, I am friends with the sachem of the tribe near my home in Sakonnet. The sachem told me that King Philip had threatened her. He said that if she didn't join him in his war, he would send his men secretly over to kill the English cattle and burn their houses. Then the English would think that she was responsible for it and attack her people."

"She didn't really want to go to war against the English, but she was later drawn into the fight. I think that a number of tribes did not want to have anything to do with this war and have been drawn into it one way or another. In fact, I've even heard that an Indian from the Connecticut River Valley tried to assassinate King Philip for starting this whole war in the first place!"

"So you think that this whole horror could have been avoided if our leaders had handled things differently?" asked Uncle Ben.

"I think King Philip would still have attacked us. He seemed bent on war. But I think that if we had been quicker to reassure some of the other Indian tribes that we want peace, this would have been over much more quickly than it will be," said Master Church quietly.

"Well, I'm not so sure that our actions at the swamp helped things," said Uncle Ben. "I think we may have just driven the Narragansetts completely over to the enemy by attacking them at the swamp, whereas before they may have been content to mostly stay out of things."

"It's hard to say," said Master Church. "Some say that the Narragansett leaders were just biding their time and waiting to attack us in the spring, while others say that they were trying to stay out of it. We do know that at least some of their warriors were helping Philip, so the tribe wasn't completely uninvolved in the war."

Finn couldn't hold back anymore. "Whatever they did or didn't do, it is no excuse for setting their wigwams on fire and killing their women and children!" he exclaimed angrily.

Uncle Ben looked at him sadly. "You're right Finn, just like there is no excuse for them killing our women and children, which they have been doing since last summer. Both sides are inflicting terrible damage upon each other."

Finn stared at him, eyes wide with fear. If both sides were killing women and children, Ginny was in horrible danger.

7

The Hungry March

Finn was growing desperate. Because of the war, it was too dangerous for him to go out on his own to look for Ginny, and time was passing. The longer it took to find her, the more chance there was that he would be transported back to the future without her. The wounded men had been moved to Newport, Rhode Island, and he had gone with them to search for Ginny there. But he'd been in Newport now for about a month, and he was anxious to leave.

One morning, Benjamin Church came limping into the room. "Finn, I think your troubles are over! General Winslow is ordering the army to head north. He's heard that the Narragansetts are starting to move, and he wants to cut them off before they can join King Philip's allies, the Nipmucks. We'll be leaving in just a few days, and you can travel with us to search for your sister if you like."

Finn sighed in relief. Finally, he'd be able to really start looking for Ginny.

*   *   *   *

A few weeks later Finn, along with the rest of Winslow's Army, was trudging through the snow, exhausted and hungry.

"I know the officers thought we would be able to live off the land as we went along, but you'd think that they would have thought to bring a little more food with us," Finn grumbled to himself.

The Narragansetts fleeing ahead of them had eaten what little food there was to be found under the winter conditions, so Winslow's army was slowly starving. Winslow's goal of stopping the Narragansetts before they could join with the Nipmucks was a colossal failure.

"Well, at least I've had a chance to search for Ginny along the way. I just wish that I had found her. Time is going by so fast. I don't know what I'm going to do if I don't find her before the time machine sends me home." His eyes filled with tears and he angrily wiped them away. *"Don't give up now Finn, that's not going to help Ginny,"* he scolded himself. *"We'll be in Boston soon. Maybe I'll find Ginny there."*

Benjamin Church rode up alongside Finn. He still hadn't fully recovered from his injuries, but had decided to come along on the march in spite of that. Uncle Ben had stayed back in Newport to recover.

"Finn, I've been thinking. Things around here are just going to get more and more dangerous. First chance I get, I'm going to find my wife and son and take them to Aquidneck Island in Rhode Island. If you ever manage to find your sister, you can bring her there too. I think it will be the safest place for you both. Just ask around town and you'll be able to find me."

Finn looked up at him. "Thank you, sir. I just hope I can find Ginny and bring her there."

Master Church looked away and then gave him a nod and rode off. Finn wondered if Benjamin Church thought finding Ginny was a lost cause.

8

Attack!

Ginny was spending the night at the Rowlandson house, which was also one of the town garrisons—a place where the people of Lancaster could go if the Indians attacked. Mary Rowlandson's husband, the town minister, was in Boston petitioning for more protection for Lancaster, and Mary was on her own with their three children. A number of people had decided that it was safer to stay in the garrison, so Mary had lots of work to do organizing and feeding them. Ginny was there to help her.

BANG! BANG! BANG!

Ginny sat up in bed, her heart pounding. She looked wildly around, and saw the other sleepers sitting up in confusion. The sun was just starting to come up, and the room was still dark in the early morning light. Suddenly she heard the noise again—gunfire! Everyone rushed to the windows and looked out. Several houses were burning, the smoke rising up to the sky. Off in the distance they could hear more gunfire and people screaming.

"The Indians are attacking! Gather up the muskets!" one of the men shouted.

Mary came over to where Ginny stood with wide eyes.

"Ginny, can you round up the young children and sit with them over in that corner? We need to keep them out of the way of the men."

Ginny rushed to do as she was asked and soon had the children gathered together. They stared up at her with fear in their eyes. She huddled close to them and wondered what she could do to keep them from panicking, when she was so close to panic herself. She could feel her heart pounding in her chest so hard she thought it would burst. The gunshots and shouting were getting closer and closer. "Please dear God, protect us all on this horrible day. Please protect us," she prayed aloud.

Then one of the older children shakily started singing a hymn and they all joined in.

Then the Indians were *there*, right outside the garrison. So many bullets hit the building that it sounded like hail raining on the sides of the house. Ginny and the children huddled together, and she wrapped her arms around as many of them as she could. A man not six feet away was shot and fell to the ground.

"Close your eyes children, close your eyes now!" she demanded.

The children closed their eyes, and Ginny closed hers, too. She heard another body falling to the ground, and then someone shrieked in pain.

Ginny could smell the sharp scent of wood smoke. "They're trying to set the house on fire!" screamed one of the women.

"Quick! Grab me a bucket!" yelled a man, and he bravely ran outside to put out the fire. The Indians soon relit the fire back up again.

Smoke filled the room. People were screaming and praying for mercy.

Mary rushed up to Ginny. "We've got to get out of here before the whole house burns down!" she exclaimed as she grabbed her children and ran for the door.

Ginny followed Mary and the rest of the colonists as they prepared to run out of the house. However, just as they were about to open the door, a rain of bullets hit the side of the house. Ginny peered through the front window and saw a large group of Indians outside, waiting to attack them as they came out. The colonists hesitated, but another cloud of smoke came billowing toward them. So, coughing from the smoke, they rushed out the door into the gunfire of the waiting Indians.

People were running and screaming, musket balls were flying. Ginny froze in panic. A man suddenly yelled and fell down dead at her feet. Ginny screamed and ran past him, just in time to see Mary's nephew, William, get hit on the head with a hatchet.

Then, Ginny heard Mary give a gasp of pain as a spot of blood appeared on her side. The child in Mary's arms started screaming, and Ginny realized that a bullet had hit both mother and child. She grabbed the hands of the two older children and ran alongside Mary until some Indians stepped out and grabbed them. One Indian pulled the two children from Ginny and turned to take them away.

"Mother, Mother, help us!" screamed Mary's daughter.

"Be brave, children," called Mary tearfully. "God will watch over you. Be brave."

Mary and Ginny looked on in horror as the two children were led away, screaming for their mother. Mary was in shock, clutching her wounded daughter to her.

Their captor turned to them. "Come with me. You won't be hurt as long as you come quietly."

Ginny and Mary looked at each other and stumbled after him. They were alive, but captured as slaves.

9

Captured!

That night Ginny sat next to Mary and her little six-year-old daughter, Sarah, and tried to help them get comfortable as best she could. But both of them were in bad shape. Poor Sarah had been hit in the stomach by the bullet, and Mary had been hit in the side.

They were camped on a hill overlooking the destroyed town. The Indians were nearby singing and dancing around a fire, having a feast on the farm animals that they had plundered from Lancaster. Of the thirty-seven people who had been in the Rowlandson house, only one had escaped. Twelve people had been killed, and twenty-four had been captured as slaves.*

---

*Accounts vary

Mary sat desolate with her poor little girl in her lap. She hadn't seen her eleven-year-old son Joseph, or her ten-year-old daughter, Mary, since they had been taken away from her. She had just watched her sister, brother-in-law, and four nephews die as they tried to escape from the burning house. Ginny huddled next to her as they tried to keep warm. She was still in shock over what had just happened and was numb with fear and the horror of what she had seen. She had no idea where they were going to be taken.

How would Finn ever find her now?

* * * *

The next morning both Mary and Sarah looked much worse. One of the Indians took Sarah up on his horse while Mary and Ginny walked behind. They could hear poor little Sarah up on the horse moaning and crying.

"I shall die, I shall die, I shall die."

Finally, Mary couldn't stand listening to her suffering anymore, so she took Sarah from the Indian and carried her in her arms while she walked. Ginny could see that Mary was getting weaker and weaker, and she tried to help her as they walked, but after a few miles Mary collapsed from exhaustion.

Ginny tried to pull her up. "Mary, let me carry Sarah for a while. Please get up, Mary. I'm afraid that they will kill you if you don't get up," she pleaded.

Just then one of the Indians came over leading a horse. He helped Mary to mount and placed Sarah in her lap. Ginny trudged along behind them, trying to tune out Sarah's moans. She had no idea where they were going, and she was exhausted from hunger and fear.

They started walking down a steep hill when Ginny heard Mary cry out. She looked up to see Mary and Sarah slide off the front of the horse and land on the ground. Sarah was crying, and the Indians nearby laughed at their plight. Ginny rushed to help them, and then her anger and frustration at everything she had experienced welled up in her. She lost her temper.

"Leave them alone," she yelled at the laughing men. "What kind of people are you anyway?"

This just made them laugh even more.

"Hush, child, it's all right," said Mary. "Don't aggravate them. I feel a bit better now and will try walking some more."

"Let me at least help you carry Sarah for a little while," begged Ginny.

Mary looked at her sadly. "I fear that I will not have many more chances to hold my child in my arms. She is no burden for me."

Tears sprang to Ginny's eyes and she nodded. They kept on walking. Soon it began to snow, and after a while they stopped for the night. Ginny, Mary, and Sarah spent the night huddled by a small fire, trying to sleep on the hard, cold ground.

They had not eaten since their capture.

10

A Sad Night

The following afternoon they reached their destination: the great Nipmuck encampment of Menameset. The Nipmucks were major allies of King Philip and the Pokanokets, and this encampment held more than two thousand people.

As Ginny walked behind the horse carrying Mary and Sarah, she looked around the encampment in despair.

"We'll never escape from here," whispered Ginny. "And Finn will never be able to find me."

Ginny and Mary were directed to the wigwam of their new master, a Narragansett leader named Quinnapin. He had purchased Ginny and Mary from the Naragansett man who had captured them.

Once they were inside their new master's wigwam, Mary and Sarah sat in a feverish stupor while Ginny tried to get them to drink some cold water—the only sustenance they'd had since their capture. Suddenly they heard an English voice outside.

"Hello in there! May I come in?"

Ginny poked her head out the door and saw an English man in torn clothing standing outside.

"Yes, please do come in, sir," she said.

The man came inside and sat down by Mary and Sarah. He had some oak leaves in his hand.

"Mistress, my name is Robert Pepper. I heard of your plight and asked permission to try to help you. I myself was wounded when I was captured many months ago, and I found that laying oak leaves on the wound helped me to recover. I have brought some for you to try."

Mary looked up at him in gratitude. "Thank you, sir, for your kindness. I am Mary Rowlandson, wife of John Rowlandson, minister at Lancaster, and this is my young relative, Ginny, and my daughter, Sarah.

Master Pepper looked down worriedly at Sarah, who was red and feverish, moaning in pain.

Mary looked up at him, and her eyes told him she knew that her daughter did not have long to live. He handed her the oak leaves, nodded quietly, and left the wigwam.

Ginny and Mary ripped pieces of their undergarments and bound the oak leaves to Mary's side and Sarah's stomach. The leaves did seem to help Mary, but they had no effect on Sarah.

* * * *

The next few days blended together as Mary and Ginny tended to poor Sarah. Nothing they did seemed to help.

The only comfort or help they received from their captors was when one or another would come in and say, "Your master will quickly knock your child on the head."

Ginny didn't know if this was meant as a threat to try to make them quiet Sarah or an offer to put her out of her misery, like a wounded animal.

Mary and Sarah were moved into a more private wigwam, and that night poor little Sarah died in her mother's arms.

11

A New Relation

Finn had been searching for Ginny in Concord all morning, when he heard someone call his name.

"Finn, is that you?" the stranger exclaimed. "Whatever are you doing here?"

"He must be another ancestor of ours," Finn thought to himself as he looked up at the man. *"It's nice to see a friendly face, but I hate having to try to figure out who these ancestors of mine are!"*

"Yes, it's me," Finn replied. "I'm here searching for Ginny. She's been missing for over two months now, and I've been going from town to town trying to find her."

"Ginny is missing?" The man looked shocked. "Has she been captured by Indians?"

"I don't know," said Finn. "I have no idea where she is."

"This is horrible news. Let us see what we can do to help you. Why don't you come and stay at our house, and we can come up with a strategy to help find her. We live just over there." The man pointed.

Finn felt a surge of relief. He was hungry and exhausted, and he had been worried about where to stay the night. Maybe this new relative would have some ideas about how to find Ginny.

"Thank you, sir, I would really appreciate that."

They walked up to the door of a small, tidy house, just as a smiling middle-aged woman opened it.

"There you are, John. I was wondering where you had gotten to." She looked over at Finn. "And who might this be?"

"Alice, I'd like you to meet my young nephew, Finn," the man replied. "His sister, Ginny, has been missing for two months now, and he is searching for her. Finn, this is my wife, your Aunt Alice."

"Oh, you poor thing," the woman tutted in concern. "Don't you worry now. We will help you find her."

Sudden tears filled Finn's eyes. How hard the last two months had been, searching for Ginny on his own! He blinked quickly, and his new Aunt Alice looked away, pretending not to see.

Aunt Alice looked at her husband and saw the same determination to help Finn in his eyes that she felt herself. Finn was no longer alone in his search for Ginny.

Later, after the evening meal, Finn and Uncle John sat in the parlor of the cozy home.

"Tomorrow you'll have to look at the new home we're building, Finn. It's for the Praying Indians under my care."

"Praying Indians?" asked Finn.

"Local Indians who have converted to Christianity," answered Uncle John. "Last November they were in dire straits, with almost no food or fuel. I was asked by the town to help care for them. There are fifty-eight men, women, and children living here. We've almost finished a workshop for them, and they've staying there at night. I lock them in as much for their own protection as to ease the fears of the townspeople. With this awful war going on, everyone is on edge."

Finn finally felt comfortable enough to ask the question that had been bothering him ever since he had arrived in this time period. "How did this war start anyhow? I mean what actually triggered it?"

Uncle John sighed. "That is a good question, Finn, but not an easy one to answer. For most of us, Indian and Englishman alike, we have gotten along fairly well through the years. We've lived as neighbors, traded with each other, and called

each other friend. However, there are always
some people who dislike anyone different from
them, both Indians and Englishmen. And there
are always people who will try to take advantage
of others if they feel they can get away with it."

Finn nodded. Even in his time there were
people like that.

"When the Pilgrims first came here, Edward
Winslow and the leader of the Pokanokets, Massasoit, became great friends who trusted each
other and treated each other with respect. They
understood that they needed each other to survive.* But then Edward Winslow and Massasoit
died, and their sons became leaders. The sons
were not as wise as their fathers were. They in-
sulted each other and did not give each other the
respect that they deserved. Massasoit's son, Alexander, broke agreements his father had made,
selling land to other colonies that he had agreed
not to sell, and not giving up land that he *had*
agreed to sell.

"Josiah Winslow, instead of treating Alexander like the leader that he was, treated him like
a wayward child or a servant, and ordered him to
a meeting in Duxbury, even threatening him
with a pistol. Alexander finally agreed to go to
the meeting, and it actually might have helped

---

*For more information on this read *The Pilgrim Adventure,*
the first book in the *Our America* series

matters, except that Alexander became ill soon after the meeting and later died.* Alexander's brother, Philip, who became the new leader of the Pokanokets, blamed the English, in particular Josiah Winslow, for his brother's death.

"Time went on and the distrust between Philip and the leaders of Plymouth grew worse. Then one day, Sassamon, a Christian Indian who had attended Harvard College, visited Josiah Winslow, who was now governor of Plymouth Colony. Sassamon told Governor Winslow that Philip was asking other tribes to join him in a war against the English. Winslow didn't want to believe him. Sassamon then told Winslow that if anyone found out he had spoken to Winslow about this, his life would be in danger.

"Not long after, Sassamon was found dead. An Indian came forward and said he had seen three other Indians murder Sassamon. The three men were put on trial and found guilty of Sassamon's murder. This trial only fueled Philip's anger, especially since these three men were his followers."

"Philip's preparations for war continued. Rumors say there was a prediction that the only way Philip would win the war would be if the English spilled the first blood. So the Indians decided to start burning the English houses and

---

*One modern doctor has suggested that Alexander might have had an appendix attack.

killing their livestock until the English retaliated.

"They got their wish in Swansea when an English boy shot at a group of Indians who were looting a house. The war had started."

Uncle John fell silent for a few moments. Then he said, "Unfortunately in times like these no one knows whom to trust. The Pokanokets make up only about five percent of all of the tribes here in New England, but now the English aren't inclined to trust any Indian, even the ones who don't want to have anything to do with the war, like the ones I am caring for. This war is hurting all of us, Indian and English alike. We are slaughtering each other like cattle."

Finn sat frozen in shock. How awful it all was, and what an opportunity had been lost for these two cultures to live together peacefully instead of living as enemies. He remembered what it had been like when the Pilgrims first came to America and how wonderful it had been to be friends with their Indian neighbors.* To see that friendship fall apart in just fifty years was a horrible tragedy.

The Pilgrim Adventure

12

An Encounter with Moseley

The next morning Finn was having breakfast with his new Aunt and Uncle when they heard a loud pounding at the door.

"I wonder who that could be," said Uncle John.

Aunt Alice looked up worriedly. "It sounds like trouble to me."

Uncle John opened the door and looked out in astonishment at a crowd of people with Captain Moseley at their head. "What is the meaning of this?" he demanded.

"We've come to make sure that your Praying Indians are all accounted for," announced Moseley.

"So many of you? Surely you didn't need to

bring half the town with you to count my Indians."

"That will be enough of that. Stop talking and just show me where they are," demanded Moseley.

Uncle John gave Moseley a hard stare and then abruptly turned and walked away. "They are over here," he said over his shoulder.

Mosley and two of his soldiers followed Uncle John to the building where the Indians lived. Finn trailed along behind. He could see the scared faces of the Indians, many of them women and children, looking out at the soldiers.

"Here they are, all present and accounted for," stated Uncle John flatly.

Moseley looked narrowly at Uncle John. "I'm going to leave a corporal and some soldiers here to secure them," he said curtly.

"There is no need for that, as you can see they are already secured," said Uncle John in exasperation. "That is what the council has commissioned me to do. These are industrious, God-fearing, quiet people. They do not need soldiers to watch them."

"Nevertheless, my soldiers are staying," Moseley said as he left the building. "And there is nothing you can do about it."

After Captain Moseley left, Finn and his uncle went back inside to finish their interrupted breakfast.

"This is the second time that I've seen Captain Moseley," Finn mentioned. "He was also at the Great Swamp Fight. If it weren't for him, I think Benjamin Church would have been able to convince General Winslow not to burn the Indians' wigwams, and the wounded men would have been able to rest a night before the long hike back."

"Well, it doesn't surprise me that the captain would want to burn down wigwams," replied Uncle John. "He has an extraordinary hatred of any Indian. Christian, non-Christian, friend, or enemy—he doesn't distinguish between them. However, I will say one thing for him; he's a good fighter. If I were in a town under attack, I'd want him around. But I believe that his unyielding hatred of all Indians has turned many of our friends into enemies and greatly increased the size of this war."

"But what can you do about the soldiers?" asked Finn.

"There is nothing much I can do about them. If Moseley wants to have his men guard peaceful Christians, then he can do that, although it seems like a huge waste of manpower to me," replied Uncle John.

* * * *

The following morning Finn was once again sitting down for breakfast with his aunt and uncle, when they heard another pounding at the door. They all looked at each other in exasperation.

"Not again!" exclaimed Aunt Alice. "Will these people ever leave us in peace?"

Uncle John got up from the table.

"The sooner I talk to them, the sooner they will go away," he said.

Finn followed his uncle to the door. Once again, Captain Moseley stood outside.

"I have come to take your Praying Indians to Boston. Gather them up immediately," he demanded.

"I will do no such thing," said Uncle John firmly. "I have been ordered by the council to take care of them, and, unless you show me an order from the council releasing them to you, I will not let you take them."

"I have a commission to kill and destroy the enemy, which overrides your council order," replied Moseley disdainfully.

"These Indians are our friends, not our enemies," countered Uncle John, "and you have no authority over them."

"Be that as it may, I'm taking them with me whether you wish it or not," Moseley replied as he turned and headed toward the building where the Indians were. "Corporal, break down that door!"

"No! You can't do this!" yelled Uncle John as he ran after the captain. "Moseley, don't do this! They are innocent!"

Two of Moseley's soldiers jumped Uncle John from behind and held his arms, while another grabbed Finn. Finn and his uncle watched helplessly as the corporal hacked on the door with an axe. The door splintered into pieces, and the rest of the soldiers poured inside the building. Moments later they came out again, cursing and pushing the Indians ahead of them. A few of the soldiers started grabbing the Indians' few possessions as they came out the door. Finn saw tears in his uncle's eyes as he watched his friends being treated so roughly. Some of the Indians nodded at Uncle John as they walked past, their faces fearful at what was to become of them.

"Where are you taking them?" demanded Uncle John.

"First to Charlestown and then to Deer Island, where the rest of their kind are being kept," replied one of the soldiers as he pointed his gun at one of the Indians. "And good riddance to them, if you ask me."

"I didn't ask you," snapped Uncle John. "These are good people and you are doing them a great wrong."

The soldier scowled. "If you've seen all of the horrors they've inflicted on our people, you'd feel the same way."

"These people have done *nothing*. They have nothing to do with the attacks on our towns."

"They're Indians, aren't they?"

Uncle John turned to Finn. "How do you combat ignorance like that?" he asked sadly. "People like this on both sides of the war will be the death of us all."

13

Reunion

Ginny walked alongside Mary as she wandered through the Indian village, searching for her lost son. With Sarah gone, Mary was anxious to make sure that her remaining two children were still alive. She had easily found her daughter, Mary, but Mary cried every time she saw her mother, so her Indian masters would not allow the two to meet. Now Mary desperately sought her son, and Ginny was worried about her.

"Oh, Ginny, I don't know how I can bear it. My little girl has died, they won't let me go near my other daughter, and my son is lost somewhere in this vast wilderness."

"At least young Mary appears healthy," offered Ginny. "And perhaps someday we will all escape from here."

"I pray every day for that," Mary quietly replied.

Just then, they heard what to any mother is the most beautiful word in the world.

"Mama!"

Mary ran toward the small figure who appeared in front of them and gathered him into her arms. "Joseph, Joseph, you're alive!"

Tears ran down Joseph's face as he said, "I saw you get shot. I was so afraid you had died."

Then he pulled back and looked into her face. "But Sarah, where's Sarah? Is she still alive?"

Mary just shook her head, and they clung to each other in their grief.

Mary and Ginny learned that Joseph was living in another village about six miles away. His master had gone with a group of men to attack the town of Medfield, and his mistress had brought Joseph to the larger camp so he could find his mother. But he was not allowed to stay with her.

At the end of their visit Joseph said, "Now Mother, I don't want you to worry about me. I'm doing just fine. You take care of yourself and don't worry about me, and maybe someday we will be free and away from all of this."

They clung to each other one last time, and then Joseph had to leave.

* * * *

The next day Ginny was grinding corn when she heard whooping and hollering coming from the woods. People stopped work and gathered together to listen. Mary came to find Ginny.

"What is it?" Ginny asked.

"The warriors are coming back from Medfield. I believe each yell stands for an English person killed." She cocked her head and listened. "I count twenty-three."*

Then the Indians gathered in the camp and began to cheer.

Mary and Ginny looked sadly at each other. Ginny thought of the horrors of their capture and could only feel pity for the poor people in Medfield who had suffered the same thing.

A little while later they saw the warriors proudly showing the scalps from the people they had killed.

---

* Accounts vary but it may have been closer to 18 killed.

14

Moving on

One of the warriors gave Mary a Bible from Medfield, and she took great comfort in reading it. But what gave her even greater comfort was knowing that both of her remaining children were alive. While there was life, there was hope, and perhaps they would all survive this ordeal somehow. They had also found some of Mary's nieces and nephews in the camp, as well as another captive woman, Goodwife Joslin.

But soon they heard that the camp was about to split up. They would be going in a different group than Mary's children.

"Oh, Ginny, I don't know how I can bear to leave my children alone here," said Mary, as they walked to her daughter's wigwam to say good-bye.

Ginny watched Mary sadly. She had no idea what to say. At least they had been allowed to see Mary's daughter before they left.

"Mother!" a young voice cried out, and Mary's daughter ran into her mother's arms.

Ginny watched with tears in her eyes as mother and daughter gave each other one last hug. They had no idea if they would ever see each other again.

And so Ginny and Mary started on their journey, trudging through the snow into the unknown. After walking for about half a day, they came to a camp. There were no wigwams. Everyone was cold, wet, hungry, and tired—captives and Indians alike.

For four more days, the journey continued in this way. And then one day, they stopped.

"Mary," Ginny said, "do you get the feeling that we are running from something?"

Mary glanced at her. "Yes, I do. I think that the English must be near. In fact I overheard some of the men talking just now, and I believe that they are sending some warriors back to hold the English off while the rest of us go on ahead."

"If the English are close, do you think we could escape and hide until they get here?"

Mary thought about this for a minute.

"I don't know. It would be very dangerous. The warriors would still be between us and the Englishmen, and if they caught us, we would be killed for sure. I think it is safer to keep going."

Ginny sighed. "If you say so. I just don't know how my brother is ever going to find me now."

Just then they received word to keep moving—at a much faster pace this time. Ginny looked around and saw all the signs of flight: a young man carrying an old woman on his back, parents hurrying their children, and everyone carrying all of their personal possessions with them. These were people in flight for their lives.

Then, they came to a large river and stopped.

"How many people do you think are here?" asked Ginny.

"I've tried to count them, but everyone keeps moving. There are hundreds of them," sighed Mary.

Ginny and Mary watched while the men started cutting down trees to build rafts to go across the river. It took over two days to get everyone across. During that time, all they were given to eat was some broth made from a dead horse.

As they drank their broth, Mary glanced up with a smile. "Last year I would have turned my nose up at this food, but now it tastes wonderful!"

Ginny grinned back at her. "I know what you mean. I never thought that I would ever eat a horse, and not only eat it, but actually like it!"

Once everyone was across the river, they burned the temporary wigwams they had built and moved on. They later found out that the Englishmen who had been chasing them arrived soon after, but had turned back at the river.

15

The Hunt Continues

Finn looked up as Uncle John burst into the room.

"You will never believe what I just heard," he announced.

"What's that?" asked Aunt Alice.

"Well, it seems that King Philip has been wintering in New York, trying to get help from the French and gather more forces. But he made a colossal blunder! He decided to try to trick the Mohawks into becoming his allies by killing some Mohawks and pretending that the English had done it. However, one of their victims escaped and told the Mohawk leaders that Philip was to blame. The Mohawks attacked Philip and drove him away from their territory. It was a huge defeat for Philip!"

Finn looked thoughtful. "You know, that's not the first time that I've heard of Philip trying to trick someone into joining forces with him. I wonder how many people on both sides of this war have been dragged into it, either unwillingly or by trickery."

"A lot, I'm sure," replied Uncle John. "I think this war has taken many people by surprise—many innocent people who just want to live in peace, like the Christian Indians who were taken away from my home."

He looked directly at Finn. "Speaking of innocent people getting caught up in this, we need to start working on a plan to find your sister," he said as he pulled out a map of New England. "Show me where you've looked already, and then we can start searching towns that you haven't already been to."

"We?" asked Finn.

Uncle John smiled. "Yes, son, I'm going to go along with you. With the war going on it's not safe for a young boy like you to be riding around by yourself. We'll leave tomorrow to start the search. I have two horses ready to go, and your Aunt Alice will pack up some food for the journey. I'd like to have an itinerary planned out before we go, so that she knows what towns we plan to search in case she needs to get a message to us."

Finn sighed in relief. It was more than he had hoped for. Not only did he have someone to help him search for Ginny, they would be going by horseback, and could cover more ground. Almost three months had passed since he and Ginny had used the time machine, but now that Uncle John was helping him, he felt as if he finally had a good chance of finding Ginny.

16

King Philip

Ginny struggled up the steep hill along-side Mary. With the lack of food and rough walking, they were both very weak, and it was all they could do to keep from collapsing. In spite of this they kept going. They had no choice—they were slaves.

After hiking for most of the morning, they came to some deserted English fields. The Indians spread out across them to glean what they could from the frozen ground. Mary and Ginny followed suit.

"Oh no!" Mary cried, after they'd been working for a while.

"What's wrong?" asked Ginny.

"Someone just stole one of the ears of corn I had found. I only turned my back for a moment and it was gone!"

Ginny sighed in disappointment. Their mistress was barely feeding them, and with hundreds of Indians in their group, all scavenging for food, every little bit they found helped keep them from starving to death. The loss of even one ear of corn was devastating.

A little while later, after they had set up camp, a man came by carrying a basket full of horse liver.

"May we have a piece?" asked Mary.

He looked at her strangely. "Do you eat horse liver?"

"If you would give me a piece, I would like to try some."

He silently handed her a piece and moved on. Eagerly, Mary and Ginny brought the piece of liver over to the fire and laid it in the coals. But before it was even half-cooked, an Indian woman grabbed it and cut half of it off for herself. Ginny and Mary looked at each other and then hurriedly took the liver off of the coals. They went into the shadows and ate it before someone else could take the rest. Ginny licked the blood from the half raw liver from her lips. She had never tasted anything so good.

"Hunger certainly makes everything taste better," she thought.

* * * *

The following afternoon Ginny and Mary were resting after yet another long hike, when they heard a voice calling.

"Mother! Mother!" Mary's head jerked up.

"Joseph? Is that you?" she cried joyfully.

Ginny grinned as she watched the happy reunion. Mother and son were allowed a brief time together, but then Joseph had to move on with his master's family, while Ginny and Mary continued following their own master.

Eventually they crossed the Connecticut River, where the group of Indians they were traveling with was to meet up with King Philip's band. After they crossed the river, Ginny looked over and was surprised to see Mary crying. In spite of everything that had happened to her: the death of her youngest daughter, the killing of her relatives, her own injury and capture, Mary had not shed one tear until now.

"Lady, why do you weep?" asked one of the Indians.

Mary looked at him blankly for a moment. "I am afraid that you will kill me," she finally answered.

"No, none will hurt you."

And then, to comfort her, one Indian brought her a few spoonfuls of meal and another brought her some peas.

As Ginny and Mary shared the food, which was kindly given, especially because food was so scarce among the Indians at that time, Ginny asked, "Were you really crying because you were afraid that they would kill you?"

Mary was quite for a moment.

"I don't know, Ginny. I think it was more a feeling of being overwhelmed with everything and missing home so very much. I must say, though, that when he asked me why I was crying, I was a bit surprised he even had to ask, considering everything we've been through!"

At that moment, a warrior came and beckoned them over towards King Philip's wigwam. It was the largest wigwam in the camp.

"King Philip would like to meet you."

Ginny and Mary looked at each other nervously. This was the man who had started the war. What could he want with them, and, more importantly, how was he going to treat them?

After a few moments they were brought into the wigwam. They sat down awkwardly in front of King Philip.

"He doesn't look too scary," thought Ginny. *"Though you can tell he is a king somehow. He has a proud air about him, even though he looks rather tired right now. He looks like he's about the same age as my parents."*

"Would you like a smoke?" asked Philip.

Ginny was so nervous that she almost giggled. This certainly wasn't what she was expecting him to say!

"No, thank you," replied Mary. "I no longer use tobacco."

Ginny just shook her head silently, too nervous to know how to reply.

"I hear you are afraid we will kill you," Philip said kindly. "Do not be afraid of that. We have no plans to hurt you."

"I thank you for that," replied Mary cautiously.

They all sat and stared awkwardly at each other. Finally King Philip broke the silence.

"What type of work does your mistress have you doing?"

Mary pulled out her knitting needles, which she kept in the pocket in her skirt, and showed him some stockings that she was making for their mistress.

Philip examined them closely and then looked back at Mary. "Could you make my son a shirt like this?"

"Yes, certainly," replied Mary.

"If you do, I will pay you a shilling for it," he replied.

Later, Ginny turned to Mary as they left the wigwam.

"He was actually nice," she said.

Mary looked at her.

"Perhaps he does have a nice side to him. But he is still responsible for the slaughter of many

English men and women, and ultimately for the death of my daughter. I will pray for him, like I do for everyone caught up in this horrible war, but I can't help remembering that he started this war in the first place."

"What about Governor Winslow?" asked Ginny. "Shouldn't he have some of the blame?"

"Maybe we all should have some of the blame," admitted Mary, "for not being considerate enough of each other. But that does not excuse anyone from murder," she said fiercely. "My little daughter was murdered. My nephews were murdered. My sister was murdered. I don't care how *nice* Philip is. He is still responsible for their deaths."

17

Another Relation

Finn looked worriedly at his uncle as they rode into the town of Rehoboth. Uncle John's face was flushed and his eyes were glassy. He'd been getting sicker and sicker over the last few days, and Finn knew that they needed to find a place to stay until Uncle John could recover. They had been searching the towns east of Concord on a north-south line for the last three weeks.

"*Well,*" thought Finn, "*I may not know where Ginny is, but I do know where she isn't—she isn't anywhere we looked.*"

He sighed as he looked around the town. And then it happened again.

"Finn, is that you?"

"*How many ancestors do I have back in this time period anyway?*" he thought. Then his face brightened. *"Maybe this is it; maybe this is the ancestor that Ginny ended up with!"*

"Finn, it's your Uncle John! Don't you recognize me?"

"Another Uncle John! This is going to get confusing," Finn thought as he smiled down at the elderly man in front of him.

"Hello, Uncle John, it is good to see you! Allow me to introduce my other Uncle John to you."

"Ahh, an uncle from your mother's side of the family I presume."

The man looked up at Uncle John's flushed face. "My name is John Kingsley, and any relative of young Finn's is welcome in my home, sir. You look as if you could use a resting place, if I might be so bold."

"John Hoar at your service," said Finn's first Uncle John in a weak voice. "And yes, we would be pleased to take you up on your kind offer."

"Sir, have you heard any word of my sister, Ginny?" Finn asked anxiously.

"Ginny? No we haven't seen nor heard from her," John Kingsley replied with a frown. "This is awful news though. Was she captured by Indians?"

Finn's heart sank. He had so hoped that maybe with this new ancestor his search for Ginny was at an end.

"We have no idea where she is. Uncle John has been helping me search for her, but we haven't had much luck so far," Finn replied.

That night, with Uncle John tucked up in bed, Finn sat down with John Kingsley and his wife, Mary.

"I need to keep searching for Ginny," said Finn. "Would it be all right if I left Uncle John with you while I continue my search?"

Aunt Mary looked at him worriedly. "It is very dangerous to leave the town right now. I think you should stay here until things quiet down some."

"I know it's dangerous, but I have to find her. I'll be careful," begged Finn. "If Uncle John can stay with you, I will search the nearest towns and then keep checking back here to see how he is doing."

"Of course he can stay with us," replied John Kingsley. "We'll help you in any way we can."

"Great! Then I'll set out tomorrow morning at first light," said Finn in relief. At least now Uncle John would have someone to care for him. He'd heard that there was a dangerous flu going around and he was afraid that was what Uncle John had.

18

Caught in a Trap

"Hey, boy, what are you doing out here?"

Finn looked up at the sound of the voice calling him. His horse, Betsy, had begun limping pretty badly, so he had stopped to check her leg. He looked up to see an Indian man wearing English-style clothing walking towards him. Finn's heart started pounding.

"You shouldn't be here, boy, it's not safe. Enemy Indians have been spotted nearby," the man said."

"I'm searching for my sister, sir," replied Finn. "I've been going from town to town looking for her."

The man looked sympathetic.

"Be that as it may, son, it's not safe here. You should to Rehoboth immediately. Or better yet, travel with us until we've checked this area to make sure it is safe, and then go back."

"Us?" asked Finn.

The man gestured behind him, and Finn saw a group of about seventy or eighty* colonial and Indian soldiers come trudging around the corner. They were all carrying muskets and looked ready for a fight. "We're hunting the enemy," the man explained.

Finn looked glumly at his horse. "I think I'll take you up on that offer, sir. It appears that my horse has gone lame, and I'll have to go back to Rehoboth anyhow."

Finn got in line with the rest of the men, leading his horse as he went. *"Another day wasted,"* he thought. *"How will I ever find Ginny at this rate?"*

Suddenly there was a commotion at the front of the line. Finn looked up and saw some of the men running forward.

"Indians ahead! Push forward, men!"

The man next to Finn turned and said, "Why don't you wait here, son. We'll come and get you once it's safe up ahead."

Finn nodded and the man rushed forward. Up ahead he could hear more yells and then shots were fired. He stood nervously next to his horse, not sure what to do. His horse was too lame to

---

*Accounts vary

ride, so he couldn't just jump on it and ride out of danger.

His decision was made for him. The shouting grew louder and he saw the men running back towards him, followed by hundreds of yelling Indians. Finn dropped the reins and ran for his life, along with the soldiers. They hadn't gone far when they were confronted by another group of several hundred Indians. Now Finn and the soldiers were completely surrounded; eighty men surrounded by almost a thousand.

"Form a circle, men! Quickly now!"

The men formed a circle and one of them pushed Finn into the center.

"Stay here, boy. Maybe if we're lucky the reinforcements will get here. In the meantime, keep your head down."

Finn crouched down. All he could see was the men's backs as they faced their enemies. For a brief moment there was silence. Then, chaos erupted. The air was filled with the screams of the dying and wounded. Men were getting killed all around him. It seemed to go on forever.

Suddenly, the man who had told him to crouch down dropped to the ground next to him. Finn could see that he was dead. His musket was laying by his side. Finn picked it up, but it was different from the muskets he'd learned to use while he was living with the Pilgrims.

"I've got to do something. I've got to help them. They're being slaughtered, and I'm going to die with them."

He picked up the gun and looked around him to see how the soldiers were using theirs. Then he jumped up and fired the musket.

Nothing happened. The musket didn't shoot.

As he was trying to figure out what was wrong, he saw something moving out of the corner of his eye. And then....darkness.

19

Escape!

Finn groaned and his head swirled as he tried to sit up. All around him he could hear yelling and screaming. *"Where Am I?"*

Then he remembered—he was in the middle of an Indian ambush! He looked around him. Dead and dying soldiers and Indians covered the ground. There were probably only about twenty soldiers left from the original eighty; the rest had all been killed.

Finn started scrabbling around looking for a weapon, anything to help him. *"I've got to get out of here."* The screams grew louder as the remaining soldiers were pressed closer together.

Finn staggered to his feet and a man grabbed his arm. He was one of the Indian allies helping the colonial soldiers.

"Quick, boy, we're going to escape this," the man said. "You see that break in the trees? When I say run, you start running. I'm going to pretend to be an enemy Indian chasing you into the woods. Maybe we can trick them and get out of here."

Finn nodded and watched as the man crouched down and blackened his face with something from his pouch so that he looked like the attacking Indians. He looked at Finn.

"Run now!"

Finn and the Indian broke free from the fighting and took off as fast as they could, the Indian waving his tomahawk. They didn't stop running until they were far away from the fighting.

When they finally stopped for breath, Finn said, "Thank you. I would have been a goner if it weren't for you."

"We helped each other," the man replied. "We need to go back to Rehoboth to report what has happened. It's going to be a long hike back."

Finn sighed wearily. *"I don't know what Uncle John is going to say when I tell him I've lost Betsy. I hope she managed to get away. I sure wish we had her now. It's going to be a long hike back to Rehoboth."*

Finn and his new friend didn't make it to Rehoboth until late that night. When it came time to say goodbye, they silently clasped each other's hands. As he walked through the dark to the

Kingsley's house, Finn knew that he would always remember this man who had saved his life.

Finn saw a light in the Kingsley's window. *"I wonder why they are up so late. I sure hope Uncle John hasn't gotten any sicker."*

"Finn, what happened to you?!" exclaimed Aunt Mary as she opened the door. "You're bleeding!"

Finn told them his story while she tended to his sore head. "I'm sorry that I lost Betsy, Uncle John," he said ruefully.

Uncle John grinned. "Well, actually you didn't lose her! She found her way home a couple of hours ago. We've been waiting for it to get light so that we could begin searching for you. We can all stop worrying now that you're home safe and sound." He gave a big yawn. "I think it's time for all of us to get some rest."

Little did they know that they weren't going to have much time to rest.

20

Fires!

Finn was worried. Uncle John was almost recovered from his illness, but Finn's new uncle, John Kingsley, had now also caught the flu, and he was not doing very well. Finn had heard about people dying of this flu, and he was very afraid that John Kingsley would be one of them.

Most of the town had moved to the local garrison after word of the Indian ambush. Now they were crowded together with the rest of the town, and all of this excitement wasn't helping the sick man recover. Finn and Aunt Mary were taking turns tending to him, but he was very feverish and seemed to be in a lot of pain.

On top of this, Finn was anxious to start searching for Ginny again. It was getting closer and closer to the time when the time machine would send him back, and if he didn't find her soon, she would be trapped here in this horrible time in history.

They were just settling down for the night when they heard some shouting in the distance.

"They're here! The Indians are here!" someone shouted.

The men grabbed their weapons and waited. They could smell the smoke of burning buildings and hear the sounds of gunfire, but the Indians never came any closer. All night the townspeople stood and anxiously waited for an attack that never came.

The next morning, they found the town destroyed. Almost every building had been burned to the ground. The townsfolk had lost everything they owned. Their homes, their livestock, their food. Nothing was left. It was late winter and it would be a few months before they could even plant any crops.

Aunt Mary was in shock. "What are we going to do? How are we going to survive?"

Her elderly husband looked up from his sickbed. "I will write to my friend, Thomas Hooker, and see if he can help us. We'll find someone to deliver the letter for us. Maybe Finn and John can start it on its way when they continue on their journey."

Excerpt from John Kingsley's Letter to His Friend, Thomas Hooker

"....I nowe, in my sicknes that the Lord hath laid on vs as hee did on Job. I am now in a fever or ague...I can say truly that since ovr waryes begun my flesh is so gon with feare, care and grife and now this sickenes, my skin is redey to cleave to my bones....Now to tel you what we have and how wee are like to sufer. My hart wil not hould to write and sheetes would [not] contayne. I am not able to beare the sad stories of ovr woeful days. When the lord made ovr wolfish heathen to be our lords. To fier our towne....they burnt our miles, brake the stones, ye, our grinding stones; and what was hid in the erth they found, corne and fowles, kild catel and tooke the hind quarters and left the rest, yea, all that day the Lord gave lisones [license], they burnt cartes wheles, drive away our catel....Now to leave all ovr danger, fear of sord, famen stares vs in the face....If aney that here or reeds wil trvst mee won barel of indien meal and won of wheat, I do promise to pay, I or mine, whe the Lord shall tvrn to his people with justice.

If any known or here that Enoes Kingsley be alive, at northampton, lett know that I his father am alive tho no shelter for my grey head, onely with won swine God left when hee sent our enemyes to be ovr lords, and blesed be his holy name hee gave a hee tooke I prayed sevn years to be fited to sufer comon calamity so the thing I fearyd is com on mee; but alas I am redey to fant in the day of adversetey and show my strength is smal."

21

News

"Finn, come quickly! There's a letter here from Concord."

Finn hurried into the garrison. They were all still staying there after the Indians had burned the town. Uncle John looked gravely at Finn.

"Finn, your Aunt Alice has written us from Concord. A soldier just gave me the letter."

Finn's heart pounded.

"Son, she says that she received a letter from a friend of mine, Jonathan Whitcomb, who says that Ginny has been staying with him and was wondering if I had heard of your whereabouts."

Finn gave a huge sigh of relief. "She's safe, then."

"Better sit down, son, there's more."

Finn sank into a chair, eyeing Uncle John warily. A cold lump formed in his stomach. "What do you mean, there's more?"

"Well, you see Finn, this letter was written a while ago. It took a long time to get to us because of the war. The problem is, Jonathan Whitcomb lives in Lancaster."

Finn sat still for a moment. "Lancaster....Do you mean that Ginny was there when Lancaster was attacked?"

Uncle John silently nodded his head. Then he leaned over and grasped Finn's hand. "But don't lose hope, son. Not all of the garrisons in Lancaster were destroyed. There is still a chance that Ginny is safe. We'll have to leave immediately and see if we can track down what happened to her. At least now we have a place to start looking."

"So we'll be leaving for Lancaster then?" asked Finn.

"No, actually we'll be leaving for Boston. I've heard that the townsfolk have recently abandoned Lancaster. They've burned down the rest of the houses themselves and moved away. They were too afraid to keep living there after the attack. I've heard that some of them have moved to Boston, so we'll go there to see if we can find word of Ginny."

* * * *

A few days later, after much searching, Finn and Uncle John tracked down Reverend Joseph Rowlandson, Mary Rowlandson's husband. Reverend Rowlandson had been visiting Boston to try to get more military help for Lancaster, when the news of his wife's capture reached him.

"Ginny, yes, she lived with the Whitcombs for about two months. I met her before I left for Boston." He sighed heavily. "I heard that she was staying at my house when it was attacked."

Finn closed his eyes, "*No, not Ginny, please God, not Ginny....*"

"It seems she was captured by the Indians, along with my wife."

Finn opened his eyes. "Captured?"

"Yes. The Indians killed many of the people in the house, but a number of them were captured. We don't know how many of them are still alive, or exactly where they are right now, but we are working on finding and freeing them somehow."

"How do you plan to do that?" asked Uncle John.

"We're trying to ransom the captives. But we're having a hard time finding anyone to bring the message to the Indians. We thought it would be safer if an Indian brought the message, and we've asked the Praying Indians on Deer Island if anyone there would be willing to try, but so far, no one has volunteered."

Uncle John thought for a moment. "Perhaps I can help you with that."

22

Hardships

Mary's knitting skills were helping keep both her and Ginny alive. She knitted stockings or caps for the Indians, and they paid her with things like bear meat or peas. Mary showed Ginny how to knit also, so between them they were able to make quite a few items.

Without this skill, Ginny often thought that they would have starved to death. Their mistress, Weetamoo, rarely fed them. Many times they were forced to go from wigwam to wigwam begging for food. They never knew what kind of reception they would get. Sometimes they were treated with kindness and given a bit to eat, and other times they were driven back out into the cold with nothing.

One day a woman gave them a piece of raw bear meat, but they were afraid to cook it in their own wigwam because their mistress might take it from them. So Mary carried the piece of raw meat around in her pocket until the next day, when they went back and asked the woman who had given it to them to help them cook it. And so it went, on and on, every day a fight for survival. And then one day, Mary heard that her son was staying about a mile away at another camp. Their master gave them permission to go visit him.

As Mary and Ginny walked through the woods, Ginny said, "I'm surprised that they let us go alone to see your son. What if we tried to escape?"

"We are so far from civilization that I don't think they're too worried about that," replied Mary. "I have no idea which direction to run in, do you?"

"I guess you're right," sighed Ginny, but she was worrying about how much time had passed. She had no idea how much time was left before Finn and the time machine were sent home. For all she knew, they were already gone, and she was trapped here. A tear rolled down her cheek.

Mary looked at her in concern. "Ginny, dear, don't cry. We'll get out of this somehow, I know we will."

Ginny sniffed. "I know. It's just that I miss my brother, and I don't know how he's ever going to find me."

Mary looked at her solemnly. "Have faith, Ginny, you must have faith."

Ginny sighed and looked around. "Mary, I really think that they don't have to worry about us running away. We can't even find a camp that's a mile away—I think we're lost!"

Mary looked around. "You know, I think you're right! I have no idea where we are going, but this certainly doesn't look like a camp to me! At least we can follow our tracks back to our own camp."

Dejected, they went back to their camp. Their master shook his head at them in exasperation, but he agreed to take them to the wigwam where Mary's son was living. They found him sick with an infected sore on his side. Mary and Ginny cleaned it as best they could, and stayed with him awhile to keep him company.

Then, it was time to go. As they walked back to their camp, Ginny noticed a tear trickling down Mary's cheek. "Oh Mary, please don't cry, or I'll start again!"

Mary wiped her face. "I won't. It's just that I am so worried about my poor son, with no one to care for him, and I don't know where my daughter is at all. I don't know if she is alive, or sick, or even dead."

Ginny held her hand. "I guess we just have to do what you said before Mary, have faith."

23

Deer Island

Finn sat in the bow of the small boat as they rowed across to Deer Island. Hundreds of Christian Indians had been forced to live there, including the Indians Uncle John Hoar had been caring for before Captain Moseley took them away.

"My poor friends, forced to live on this small island with little food or shelter," mourned Uncle John. "Though I don't know how much better it would have been for them on the mainland, what with so many people prejudiced against them. I hear that over in Chelmsford the English attacked a Christian Indian village, wounding some women and children, and killing a young boy. All because they thought that the Christian Indians had burned a barn that some enemy Indians had actually burned." He sighed. "I've also heard of enemy Indians purposefully attacking places near where Christian Indians live to try to get them blamed for the outrages. And it often works. Many English have lost all trust in the Indians, because some Indians who they thought were their friends betrayed them. And many Indians have lost all trust in the English, for similar reasons. It is truly a horrible time that we're living in."

"Boy is he right. I can't wait to find Ginny and get out of here," thought Finn.

The boat scraped up onto the shore and the men climbed out.

Finn looked around. "Just how big is this island anyway?" he asked.

"Around one hundred and eight-eight acres," replied Uncle John. "Not nearly enough land for five hundred people to live on. They mostly eat clams and other shellfish. They also have a little corn, but it's not nearly enough to feed them all. Many of them are starving. It's a crime that they have been treated so poorly. And these people are our friends, not our enemies."

They walked up a path that led to an encampment of wigwams. Uncle John asked around for his friends who had been taken from his home in Concord, and soon they were led into the wigwam of a man named Tom Nepponit.

The two men shook hands. "Tom, I am sorry to see you here. I wish that you were still living in Concord with us," said Uncle John.

"We are still much better off than the poor souls who have been here all winter," replied Tom. "They have had to endure this many more months than we have." He turned to Finn. "I remember you from when we were taken from Concord—you tried to help us. I thank you for that."

"Finn is actually the reason we've come here today," said Uncle John. "His sister was captured when Lancaster was attacked. We're looking for someone to go to the enemy to ransom her and the other captives before any harm comes to them."

Tom pondered this for a while. Then he said slowly. "I believe that I am up for that venture. You will have a much better chance of success if an Indian tries to approach them rather than an Englishman."

Finn sat back in relief. Now that Tom Nepponit had offered to help them, he felt that Ginny had a real chance of being set free.

* * * *

A couple of weeks later Finn was anxious. It had been about nine days since Tom Nepponit had gone off into the wilderness to try to ransom Ginny and Mary. Now that he knew where Ginny was, it was harder to just sit and wait for someone else to find her. Plus, this horrible war seemed to have no end in sight. Every day it seemed as if there was word of another attack or atrocity committed by one side or the other.

They'd just found out that the great Narragansett warrior sachem, Canonchet, had been captured and killed by a group of Indians led by Captain Denison of Connecticut. Instead of distrusting their Indian friends, Connecticut had enlisted them to help with the war, and subsequently had come through the war with less damage than Massachusetts.

As Finn sat behind the house contemplating the sunset and wondering how people could inflict such pain on each other, he heard Uncle John calling.

"Finn, come quickly; Tom's back!"

Finn hurried into the house and stopped when he saw Tom sitting at the table, wrapped in a blanket.

His words tumbled out. "Did you find her? Is she safe?"

Tom looked up. "No, I did not see her, but I hear that she is alive and well."

Tears came into Finn's eyes and he plopped down at the table. He hadn't realized how much stress he'd been under, not knowing if Ginny was alive or dead, but suddenly it felt as if a huge weight had been lifted off of him.

"Thank you so much," he said to Tom. "Thank you."

"We've still got a long way to go," replied Tom in a tired voice. "They have not agreed to release her yet. But their answer does give us some hope that we will be able to negotiate for the captives' freedom. I'll be going back again, this time with my friend, Peter Conway."

The Response to Tom Nepponit's First Attempt to Ransom Mary Rowlandson

We now giue answer by this one man, but if you like my answer, send one more man besides this one Tom Nepanet, and send with all true heart and with all your mind by two men, because you know and we know your heart great sorrowful with crying for your lost many hundred men and all your house and all your land, and woman, child and cattle, as all your thing that you have lost and on your backside stand.

Sam Sachem
Kutquen and   Peter Jethro
Quanohit Sagamore   Scribe

Mr. Rowlandson, your wife and all your child is well but one dye, your sister is well and her 3 child. John Kettel your wife and all your child is all well, and all them prisoners taken at Nashua is all well.

Mr. Rolandson se your louing Sister his hand
Ƈ Hannah

And old Kettel wif his hand Ƭ

Brother Rowlandson, pray send thre pounds of Tobacco for me if you can, my louing husband pray send thre pound of tobacco for me.

This writing by your enemies
SAMUEL USKATTUHGUN and
GUNRASHIT. two Indian Sagamores

24

More Hardships

Things were getting worse and worse for Ginny and Mary. Their master, Quinnapin, who was a Narragansett sachem, was temporarily gone, leaving them at the mercy of their mistress, Weetamoo, who was a sachem in her own right. Weetamoo had taken a real dislike to Mary and went out of the way to make life miserable for her. Weetamoo rarely fed them, so much of Ginny and Mary's time was spent looking for food to keep from starving.

One afternoon Mary and Ginny went out to scavenge for food in the woods.

"Here are some acorns, Ginny," Mary said. "Six for you and six for me."

As they sat munching the acorns, Ginny said, "We should probably gather some wood for the fire since we're here."

They found a few chestnuts to eat while they gathered wood, and then they made their way back to the wigwam for the night. When they got there they saw that it was crowded with people.

"Go away!" demanded their mistress. "I have guests tonight, and there is no room for you here!"

"But where should we go?" asked Mary. "We have no other place to sleep, and it's cold outside."

"Go look for a place, any place, but leave here."

"But if we go to another wigwam, they might get angry with us, and send us right back here."

Then one of the men drew a sword. "If you don't leave right now, I'll run you through this instant."

At that, Mary and Ginny hurriedly left. They went from wigwam to wigwam begging for a place to spend the night. Finally an old man and his squaw let them stay in their wigwam and even gave them some nuts to eat.

* * * *

Soon they were on the move again. After they reached yet another encampment, Mary asked one of the Indians if he had seen her son.

The man sneered. "His master killed him and ate him."

Mary stared at him in horror.

"And I myself ate a piece of him," he said.

Mary sank to the ground in shock.

Ginny frowned at the man and waved him away. "Mary, don't believe him. He's just fooling you. We haven't seen anyone here eating people. They are not cannibals."

"But why would he say something like that to me?" Mary whispered

"Some people think that it is funny to hurt others. He's just one of those," said Ginny. "Try to forget about it. I'm sure that your son is fine."

That same night, as Mary and Ginny lay by the fire, Mary reached out and moved a stick to let more heat come toward her. One of the women saw what she did and moved it back. Then she reached over and threw some ashes right into Mary's eyes.

"Ahhh!" screamed Mary. "I think she's blinded me!"

Ginny rushed over and helped Mary clean her eyes with water she found near the fire. Then she held Mary as she rocked back and forth in agony.

Later, as they lay next to each other in the dark, trying to sleep, Mary whispered to Ginny, "You know, Ginny, you can learn a lot about someone by how they treat the people that work for them or are under them. Some of the people here are souls of kindness, but others are just plain hateful."

Ginny could only squeeze Mary's hand in agreement.

25

Things were somewhat better the next morning; at least Mary still had her sight, though her eyes were red and the skin around them was burned. Then, another English captive was brought in who told Mary that her husband was well, but "melancholy." This was good news since the Indians had told her at various times that he had either died or had re-married. Not too long after that, Mary heard that her son was at their encampment, alive and well. Things seemed to be looking up—that is until Mary and Ginny went to visit yet another English captive, John Gilbert. They found the boy curled up outside in the cold with only a shirt and waist coat on.

"Son, why are you outside like this?" Mary asked gently.

"I ate something that made me sick," he slurred, his voice weak. "They don't want me in the wigwam."

Mary rubbed his hands briskly. "You need to try to find another wigwam. You'll die of cold out here."

"But I cannot stand up," he protested.

"We'll help you," replied Ginny, as she and Mary helped the poor boy to his feet. They brought him to a wigwam where they knew some kindly people lived, and left him huddled up next to their fire.

As soon as Mary and Ginny were back at their own wigwam, the daughter of John Gilbert's master came storming up. "What have you done with him?!"

Mary looked at her in surprise. "With John Gilbert? I brought him to your neighbor's wigwam so that he could get warm."

"I don't believe you! Show me where he is."

So Mary and Ginny walked back and showed her where they had brought the boy.

In the meantime, rumors had run rampant through the camp. When they returned to their wigwam, their mistress demanded angrily, "Where have you been? What have you been doing? People are saying that you plan to take the English boy and run away! If you've been planning to escape, we'll knock him on the head and kill him!"

"We were just visiting him. We're not planning to run away," said Ginny bravely.

Their mistress picked up a hatchet and waved it at them. "I will knock you down if you try to leave this wigwam. You will stay here from now on!"

Ginny looked over at Mary in concern. Their mistress almost never fed them. If they couldn't leave the wigwam, they would surely starve to death.

They remained trapped in the wigwam for a day and a half. Then, a man came to them with a pair of stockings that he wanted unraveled and re-knitted to fit him.

Ginny and Mary looked at each other. This might be their chance to finally leave the wigwam. Mary said to the man, "Please ask my mistress if it would be all right for us to discuss this outside with you."

The man did, and Ginny and Mary were allowed outside. He also gave them some roasted ground nuts, which they desperately needed. From then on, they were allowed outside again.

Not long after this, Mary's son was allowed to visit her so that she could comb the lice out of his hair. Ginny was surprised at how much thinner he had gotten.

"Mother, I'm hungry. Do you have anything to eat?" he pleaded.

Mary shook her head sadly. "No, Joseph, I don't have any food here. On your way back to your master you should try asking at some of the other wigwams."

Joseph did as she suggested, but unfortunately, he took too long to return to his master, who beat him and then sold him to another Indian. Despite the beating, this was a good thing.

Joseph ran back to Mary with the news. "Mother, I have a new master, and he's given me some food to eat, and he's said that I can bring you to meet him!"

Mary and Ginny walked back with Joseph to meet his new master, who assured them that he would take good care of Joseph. No longer would Joseph go hungry. Joseph and his new master left the encampment soon after, but Mary wasn't as worried about him as she had been. She knew he was in kind hands.

26

Hope

The Indians stayed on the move from one encampment to another to elude the English. All of this traveling was hard for Ginny and Mary, who were weak from lack of food. It all came to a head one morning when they were crossing a swift-flowing river. Mary stepped in first and gasped. "The water is so cold! I feel as if it is cutting right through me!" The man in front of her impatiently motioned them forward.

Ginny apprehensively put her foot in the water and quickly jerked it out again. It was freezing! She gingerly put her foot back in and forced herself forward, watching carefully where she stepped. The swift-flowing water was soon up to her knees. That was when she heard the laughter. She looked up. In front of her poor Mary was so exhausted and weak that she couldn't walk straight in the current. She was reeling and staggering back and forth as she tried to move forward. The Indians on shore were pointing and laughing at her.

Ginny watched in horror as Mary stumbled and was almost swept downstream. "Mary wait!" she cried. "Wait until I catch up to you! We can go together." She slowly made her way to Mary and then they clasped arms and made it to the other side.

As they sat down to put their socks back on, Ginny saw tears trickling down Mary's cheeks. She started blinking her own eyes to prevent herself from crying too.

And it was at that exact moment that things started looking better. A man hurried toward them.

"You two, you must go to Wachusett, to where your master is. A letter has arrived. They are talking about a ransom to let you go free. Another letter will be arriving in fourteen days, so you need to be there by then."

Ginny and Mary smiled at each other. Suddenly the idea of getting up and walking again didn't seem as difficult as it had just a moment before.

But in spite of (or perhaps because of) their new found hope, the next fourteen days seemed to go on forever. Both Ginny and Mary were so weak that even the possibility of escape barely kept them going. When they would stop for the night, they would sink to the ground, too tired to even talk. Plus, although Ginny was relieved that they would soon be rescued, she wondered what was to become of her. Where was Finn?

Once they overnighted in an Indian town with four English children—and one of them turned out to be Mary's niece! Her owners would not let Mary and Ginny spend the night with her, but at least Mary could see that she was alive. After they left her, Ginny and Mary went from wigwam to wigwam in the town begging for food. Finally, one woman gave them each a little piece of a boiled horse hoof.

Word of their begging got back to their mistress. She greeted them angrily when they returned to her wigwam. "You disgrace your master with your begging," she scolded them. If I catch you begging again, I will knock you on the head!"

Mary pulled herself up to her full height. "You might as well knock me on the head as starve me to death! If you would feed us properly, we wouldn't have to go out and beg!"

Their mistress looked at them in disgust and stomped off.

"I can't believe that you said that!" exclaimed Ginny. "She really might have hit you!"

"No, I don't think so," replied Mary thoughtfully. "We're worth ransom money to them now. They don't want anything to happen to us."

The next day, they were trudging through a swamp, up to their knees in mud and water. King Philip, who was traveling with them, sought Mary out. He took hold of her hand as he helped her through the mud. "Two weeks more, and you shall be mistress again."

"Is this really true?" asked Mary, her eyes searching his face.

"Yes. And soon we will reach the place where your master, Quinnapin, is staying, and you can rest."

That evening, they finally reached the place where their master was. When they walked into his wigwam, he took one look at them and asked, "When was the last time you washed?"

"Not at all this month," replied Mary.

"I wonder why he is worried about this now," thought Ginny. *"Maybe it is because he wants to show the English that they've been taking care of us. Or maybe it's just because we are filthy!"*

Quinnapin got them some water to wash with, and asked one of the women in his wigwam to get them something to eat. She brought out beans, meat, and some ground nut cake.

Ginny felt as if she'd been invited to a feast. She looked up at the woman serving them. "Excuse me, but I am curious. What is your relation to our master?"

"I am Quinnapin's oldest wife," the woman replied with a smile.

Ginny was taken aback. "He has more than one wife?"

"He has three wives. I am the oldest, next is your mistress, and he also has a young wife with two children."

Just then, Weetamoo's maid ducked inside the wigwam. She turned to Ginny and Mary.

"Weetamoo wants both of you back at her wigwam right away."

Mary started to cry. "Please don't make us go back there to her. We'd much rather stay here with you."

The older wife looked kindly at her. "You need to go back to her now. But anytime you need something to eat, just come back here, and you can sleep here at night as well."

Later that night, Ginny and Mary went back to their master's wigwam. They were given a mat to lie on and a blanket. They both had tears in their eyes at these small kindnesses.

27

Negotiations

And then Uncle John Hoar's Christian Indian friends arrived: Tom and Peter, along with a letter from the council in Boston. Ginny and Mary were brought inside one of the wigwams to meet them. Mary burst into tears and could not speak for crying. When she finally calmed down, her first question was, "How is my husband?

"He is doing well," Tom answered, "but he is very melancholy and worried about you and the children."

Mary's face fell. "Does he know about poor Sarah? That she died when we were captured?"

Tom took her hands. "Yes, he knows. He's also received word that your other children are still alive and well. We are working very hard to free as many of the Lancaster captives as we can."

Then Tom turned to Ginny, who was standing off to the side. "And your brother is well too, Ginny."

Ginny stared at him in amazement. "You've seen my brother? He knows where I am?"

Tom grinned. "Yes. He has been working very hard to find you. He was one of the party that asked me to try to ransom you."

Now Ginny had tears running down her cheeks as well, and she gave Tom a huge hug. "Thank you so much, thank you."

Tom's grin faded. "It is not over yet. We are still negotiating. I doubt that they will free you immediately. You should be prepared to wait a little longer."

"I'm just happy that my brother knows where I am," said Ginny. "I was so worried that he would never find me."

A little while later Mary and Ginny were called into the wigwam where the Indian leaders were discussing the ransom.

One of the men asked Mary, "How much do you think your husband would pay to have you back?"

Mary thought for a while. Ginny knew that Mary's husband had lost everything in the fire that destroyed their home during the attack of Lancaster. It would be difficult for him to pay anything to redeem her.

Finally Mary said, "Twenty pounds."

"That's a lot of money," thought Ginny. *"But then again, if Mary chose too small an amount, maybe they wouldn't ransom her."*

Then they turned to Ginny, who had no idea how much to ask. *"But I'm younger, and probably considered less valuable."*

"Fifteen pounds," she finally said. She turned and whispered to Tom who was next to her, "But, who is going to pay my ransom? My brother doesn't have any money."

"Your uncle, John Hoar, has agreed to pay your ransom," he reassured her.

"I wonder who that is? He must be one of our ancestors that Finn met," Ginny speculated.

A Praying Indian, who had turned against the English and was now helping King Philip, wrote down their demands. Ginny and Mary had to resign themselves to another long wait while Tom and Peter took the Indians' response back to Boston.

The Response After the Second Attempt to Ransom Mary Rowlandson

For the Governor and the Council at Boston

The Indians, Tom Nepennomp and Peter Tata-tiqunea hath brought us letter from you about the English Captives, especially for Mrs. Rolanson; the answer is I am sorrow that I haue don much wrong to you and yet I say the falte is lay upon you, for when we began quarel at first with Plimouth men I did not think that you should haue so much truble as now is: therefore I am willing to hear your desire about the Captives. Therefore we desire you to send Mr. Rolanson and goodman Kettel: (for their wives) and these Indians Tom and Peter to redeem their wives, they shall come and goe very safely: Whereupon we ask Mrs. Rolanson, how much your husband willing to giue for you she gaue an answer 20 pound in goodes but John Kittels wife could not till. and the rest captives may be spoken of hereafter.

28

Waiting

"I hope that my husband does not come along with the rescue party," said Mary for what seemed the hundredth time.

Ginny could only nod in agreement. The long wait to hear back from Boston was getting on both their nerves. Mary was worried about the Indians' reactions if her husband came. Some of the Indians said that he would be safe if he came, and some said that they would hang him...and some said one minute that he would be safe and the next that he would be hanged. It was all very worrying, and Ginny could only silently hope that Finn wouldn't come either.

"But knowing Finn, he'll come along if he can," she thought.

That night, the Indians held a pow wow to help them prepare for an attack on the town of Sudbury. As she watched them beat the ground and give their speeches, Ginny could only think of the poor unsuspecting town that was about to be attacked. If only there was some way to warn them! But there wasn't, and the attack took place soon after. Then they had to move camp again, just in case the English retaliated. Some of the Indians said that after the attack on Sudbury, the English would be so angry they wouldn't want to pay the ransom for the captives. This had Ginny and Mary very worried.

At their new encampment, the Indians built a huge wigwam—large enough to hold a hundred people. They were preparing for a big day of dancing, and Indians from miles around were gathering for the dance. One of them was the master of Mary's sister, who had also been captured by Indians during the raid on Lancaster. However, neither master would let the sisters visit each other. Then Mary heard that her daughter was only a mile away, but even though she begged and pleaded, she was not allowed to visit her.

"Why won't they let me see her?" Mary wondered tearfully.

"Maybe it has to do with that twenty pounds that they hope to get for you," suggested Ginny. "They want to make sure that nothing happens to you before they collect it."

"I certainly hope that is the reason," replied Mary. "That would mean that there is still a chance that we will be ransomed."

Ginny, who was much happier now that Finn knew where she was, agreed.

29

Danger

Finn sat on his borrowed horse as it plod-
ded through the forest. Ahead of him were Uncle
John Hoar, Tom, and Peter. It had taken a lot of
convincing to get Uncle John to agree to let him
go along on this trip, but Finn was determined to
help rescue his sister. There was only a week left
until the time machine sent him back, so he
couldn't afford to wait any longer. He had to be
with Ginny when the time machine sent him
home, otherwise she would be trapped back in
time. If Uncle John was going, so was he, and
that was that. Uncle John had finally relented
when he realized that Finn would probably try to
follow them anyhow.

They had been traveling for a couple of days
now, and Finn was actually enjoying the trip.

The weather was warmer now and spring had finally arrived. Peter and Tom were teaching him lots of great survival tricks, one of the most important being how to travel quietly through the woods. If they heard even a squeak from a harness, they immediately took measures to stop it. They never forgot that they were traveling in enemy territory, and they didn't want to attract any unwanted attention.

As they approached King Philip's encampment, an Indian stepped out of the woods and pointed a musket at them. The horses halted, and then more Indians came out from where they had been hiding in the trees. Finn was nervous, but watched Uncle John and their Indian guides to see how he should react.

Then without warning, shots rang out. Some of the Indians were firing at them, but aiming above, below, and in front of their horses. In the confusion, Finn's horse started to buck, and he fought for control. The horse reared up again, and one of his hands slipped from the reins. He started to slide off, but one of the Indians on the ground grabbed the loose rein and helped him to calm the horse.

"Get off your horses, now!" ordered one of the Indians.

Finn and Uncle John quickly climbed down from their horses and watched as they were led away. The Indians crowded around them, getting closer and closer until suddenly one of them shoved Finn hard from behind. Another Indian pushed him back, and he saw out of the corner of his eye that Uncle John was being shoved from Indian to Indian also. They seemed to be leaving Peter and Tom alone. Tom gave Finn a reassuring nod.

"See what we can do to you Englishmen? You are in our power now and on our territory. Now you have to do what we say, so come with us."

Finn took his cue from Uncle John's calm demeanor and quietly followed the line of men into a nearby wigwam, where he sat down next to his uncle in a circle of Indians.

First they smoked some tobacco together, which Finn declined. *"I wonder what they would do if I told them that in the future we've learned that smoking tobacco will kill you."*

Then the men got down to business.

"I have brought another letter from the Council in Boston," said Uncle John. "I have also brought some goods as ransom for the hostages." He handed the letter to the Indians.

"What types of goods did you bring?" demanded Quinnapin.

"Food, trading cloth, and the like. Twenty pounds worth of goods for Mistress Rowlandson and fifteen pounds for the girl, Ginny." replied Uncle John.

The Indians glanced wordlessly at each other. "We will discuss this amongst ourselves and let you know our decision later. You will spend the night with us, and we will talk again tomorrow."

30

Reunion

Ginny and Mary were out gathering firewood when they were called back to camp.

"You two sit here and do not move," ordered one of the warriors. Then he grabbed his gun and ran off with some other men into the woods.

"What is going on?" wondered Ginny.

A woman who was grinding some corn nearby looked over at them. "Some Englishmen have arrived at our camp."

Ginny and Mary looked wonderingly at each other. Could this possibly have anything to do with their ransom?

Then they heard the sound of musket shots, and Ginny closed her eyes in fear. *"Please don't be Finn,"* she thought, *"Please don't let Finn be shot."*

After a while, one of the men came back and saw that Ginny and Mary were anxiously clutching each other. "What is the matter?"

"Did you kill the Englishmen?" Mary asked with a tremor in her voice.

The man laughed. "No, we didn't kill them. We just scared them a little to show them what we could do. They are meeting with our leaders now."

"Can we see them please?" begged Mary.

"No! You two are to stay here until you are called for," he said sternly as he walked away.

Ginny clutched Mary's hand and said, "They must be here for our ransom, otherwise why did they make us stop collecting firewood and sit here?"

Mary nodded, too full of hope to speak.

After what seemed like hours, Ginny saw some Indians leading four people toward them. As they got closer, her heart leapt—one of them was Finn! She jumped up, ran toward him, and threw herself sobbing into his arms.

Finn hung on to her with tears in his own eyes and said, "It's all right now, Ginny, I'm here. I've found you, and we'll be going home soon."

31

More Waiting

"Will we be able to go home now?" asked Mary.

"No, it has not been decided," answered one of the Indians.

"*Well,*" Ginny thought as she fell asleep later that night. "*At least Finn is nearby. All we need is to be together when the time machine sends us back. He said that we only have a week left, so I'm sure that we can think of some way to be together on that day.*"

The next morning Uncle John invited the Indian leaders to a meal. When he went to get the food out for it, he found that much of his food had been stolen.

Quinnapin was very upset when he heard about the theft. "I am sorry that someone stole from you. That is not right when you came here in good faith."

"Well, at least some of the ransom goods are still intact," said Uncle John. "I think we can still come to some kind of agreement."

There was still some food left, so Mary and Ginny helped Uncle John prepare the meal. They had gotten very good at cooking over a campfire during their capture.

However, the meal wasn't the main entertainment of the day. It was time for the big dance that the Indians had been spending so much time preparing for. Ginny and Finn were allowed to watch the dance, and Finn was especially excited as he had never seen anything like it before. Four men and four women got up to start dancing. One of the women was Ginny's mistress, Weetamoo, who was wearing a wool coat and was covered with bands of wampum—the beads made from shells that the Indians used for money. Her arms from her elbows to her hands were so covered in bracelets that there was no space between them, and she had on piles of necklaces. Her hair was powdered white and her face was painted red. Two Indians sang and pounded on a kettle while the eight people danced until nightfall, tossing out wampum to the audience.

That night, Mary asked again if they could go home, and again was told "no." However, later, their master sent word that he would let them go for one pint of liquor. Uncle John, who was with them at the time, quickly left the wigwam and brought back Tom and Peter to act as witnesses to the agreement. Then, Mary and Ginny's master agreed to let them go for the liquor.

The following morning a general court was held. It was agreed that Ginny and Mary could finally be released. The group wasted no time in leaving, and they were soon on their way to Boston, where Mary's husband was waiting for her.

As they rode away from the camp, Ginny kept looking back.

"What's wrong?" asked Finn.

"I keep worrying that they're going to change their minds and come after us," Ginny admitted.

Finn looked at her in concern. "Don't worry, Ginny. You're free now and it's all over."

32

Home

Tomorrow was the big day—the day that the time machine was going to take them home! Ginny and Finn couldn't wait to leave this horrible time in our country's history.

"I had no idea how bad King Philip's War was," said Ginny. "The history books don't tell us much about it in school."

"It was as if the whole world went mad and people lost all compassion and feeling for each other," replied Finn.

"I can't wait to get home," said Ginny. "But I am going to miss Mary. She and I went through so much together. It's going to be awful never seeing her again. I will never forget her."

Ginny and Finn had been staying with the Rowlandsons while Ginny and Mary recovered from their ordeal. Finn was glad to see Ginny fattening up a bit—he'd been afraid that when they got back to their own time in the future that people would wonder what had happened to her since she was so thin.

"I'm going to spend this last day with Mary," declared Ginny.

"Well, I'd like to spend my last day with Uncle John," said Finn. "I'm going to miss him when we're back home. I'm glad that he is our ancestor. I feel as if a part of him lives on in us. Isn't it great how we get to meet our ancestors this way?"

Ginny nodded in agreement. "Yes, I enjoyed my time with the Whitcombs before Lancaster was attacked. I'm glad to hear that they survived the attack."

"Let's meet up this evening and sneak out of the house before midnight, since we don't know exactly when the time machine will take us back," Finn replied

Ginny smiled at him. "Sounds like a good plan to me."

* * * *

That evening, they were outside looking up at the stars, waiting for the time machine to send them home.

Ginny looked sad as she turned to Finn.

"We've been through so much, and we still haven't found Mom and Dad."

"I know." Finn sighed. "But I'm not giving up, are you?"

"No, never," said Ginny resolutely. "After this experience, I know that I can handle anything that comes my way. I'm not giving up. We're going to find them. I just know it."

At that moment, the world started spinning, and the time machine sent them home.

Historical Notes

Finn and Ginny are fictitious characters, but all of the people from the seventeenth century mentioned in this book were real people, except for the man named "John" who helped Finn during the Great Swamp Fight. I chose the name John for him because there were a number of men with that name who participated in the fight. Also, as I mentioned in the first book of this series,* while this book is mostly based on accounts told by the people who actually lived through the events in the story, we don't know what their actual conversations were. This means that while most of the incidents in this book actually happened, the conversations associated with them are fictitious. And of course, people in the seventeenth century did not use the same speech patterns that we use today. I chose to write the book using modern speech patterns to make it easier for the young reader.

King Philip's War erupted in June of 1675 and wound down in August of 1676, when King Philip was killed. In April of 1678 the Treaty of Casco was signed in Maine, marking the final end of

---

*The Pilgrim Adventure

this tragic and horrible time in our country's history. It truly was "a world gone mad." What is particularly disturbing is how people who had lived together relatively peacefully for about half a century could so quickly ignite into violence against each other—so quickly that it seems that even the participants were shocked and confused by what had happened.

King Philip's War is typically mentioned only briefly in history books for children, possibly because it was so gruesome, or possibly because neither side in the conflict can be viewed in a very good light. It was perhaps the most brutal war ever waged within our country in terms of harm done to civilians. Both sides were guilty of horrible atrocities against not only the soldiers and warriors of the enemy, but against women, children, and the elderly. And there were many times when both sides behaved dishonorably.

However, despite the lack of educational coverage, King Philip's War's importance to the history of our country is immense. In a very short period of time, more than half the English towns in New England had been attacked. Further, a larger percentage of people (compared to the overall population) were killed in King Philip's War than in either World War II or the Civil War.

The consequences of the war for the Native Americans were even worse. Before the war, Native Americans accounted for about thirty percent of the people living in New England. After the war was over, due to deaths from the war and the Indian prisoners that were sold as slaves to the Caribbean and other locations, they accounted for only fifteen percent. This changed the whole dynamic of the region. The opportunity for the Native Americans of the region and the English to forge a way to live together in peace was lost. Too much damage had been done, and any trust between the nations was broken.

Many New Englanders of the time considered their eventual victory over the Indians as God's punishment of the Indians for not following Christianity. But before getting upset over the unfairness of this attitude, modern readers need to understand that these same New Englanders also believed that pretty much anything bad that happened to *anyone* was God's punishment for one sin or another. For example, many felt that the Indians' attacks on the English were God's punishment on the English for their sins. And in her memoirs, Mary Rowlandson expresses the thought that her own captivity is a punishment for her sins.

In *The Pilgrim Adventure,* the ancestors that Finn and Ginny meet back in time are actual ancestors not only of Finn and Ginny, but also of mine. The same holds true for this book, only this time Finn and Ginny meet a *number* of our mutual ancestors. If this were a complete work of fiction I would have been able to choose the names of my characters, but since Finn and Ginny are meeting my actual ancestors, I had to use their real names. Thus, I ran into the problem of having two "Uncle Johns" in the book. John must have been a very popular name back then! Below is a bit of information on whom these ancestors were and what happened to them after King Philip's War.

Little is known about Benjamin Webster (Uncle Ben), whom Finn meets right before the Great Swamp Fight. It is known that he participated in the fight under Lieutenant Swain and that he was wounded in the battle. He survived the war and married a woman named Grace. There is some evidence that he was a shoe maker.

Jonathan Whitcomb and his wife, Hannah, (Uncle John and Aunt Hannah), who take care of Ginny before Lancaster is attacked, also survived the war, although they lost their home and had to live elsewhere for a number of years. While I was researching them, I discovered that Jonathan actually knew John Hoar, one of the other ancestors in this book (they served together on a jury). Jonathan and Hannah had nine children together, and Jonathan eventually died in 1690. Hannah survived King Philip's War, only to be killed by Indians in 1692 during one of the French-Indian Wars.

I have to admit that I have a favorite ancestor in this book: John Hoar (Uncle John). He volunteered to take care of the Concord Praying Indians when no one else would, and he tried to keep Captain Moseley from taking them away to Deer Island. He also helped rescue Mary Rowlandson, which was an extremely brave act. John and his wife, Alice, (Aunt Alice) both survived King Philip's War and lived many more years in Concord.

My last ancestor in this book was the elderly John Kingsley. His wife, Mary, was his third wife and not an ancestor of mine. They lost their home in Rehoboth when it was attacked and were left destitute. Both he and his wife died about two years later.

Finn's experience during the attack on Captain Pierce's troops where an Indian ally pretends to chase him as a way to escape the battle is said to have actually happened. Of course, this didn't happen with Finn, but with an unknown soldier.

The descriptions of the attack on the Rowlandson home in Lancaster and of Mary and Ginny's experiences with the Indians were taken from a book Mary Rowlandson wrote about her captivity. The biggest difference between her account and this story is that Mary did not have Ginny or any other friend with her during her ordeal. After her rescue, Mary was reunited with her husband, and not long after that her son and daughter were also rescued.

Another character in the book, Benjamin Church, is often described as a Daniel Boone-like person. He was comfortable with Indian and English alike. Toward the end of the war he led the group of both Indian and English soldiers who eventually killed King Philip. He lived many years after the war and was an important figure in the French-Indian Wars.

Like Mary Rowlandson, Benjamin Church also wrote of his experiences during King Philip's War. He recorded how he met Mary and Ginny's Indian mistress, Weetamoo, at the beginning of the war. According to Church, most of Weetamoo's warriors had gone against her wishes to the war dances. At that time she appeared to be against the war, as Church advised her to let the governor of Plymouth know that she did not want to fight the English. When she met Church, Weetamoo was married to a man named Peter Nunnuit, who eventually left her and joined the English to fight against Philip. Weetamoo then married the Narragansett sachem Quinnapin, who was Ginny and Mary's master. Weetamoo drowned while crossing a river when her raft broke up, the same year that Mary Rowlandson was rescued.

Up until shortly before Mary's rescue, things looked grim for the English colonists. They had been driven from many of their towns and it seemed as if town after town was falling to the Indians. However, the Indians were also in desperate straits, and some were losing their enthusiasm for the war, particularly after one of their greatest warriors, the Narragansett sachem Canonchet, was killed. A number of the tribes had entered the war only reluctantly, and once spring came in 1676, they needed to start planting their crops again so that their people wouldn't starve. Some of these tribes quietly left the war, among them Benjamin Church's friend, the female sachem Awashonks. He convinced her to not only make peace with the English, but to help him track down King Philip.

As mentioned earlier, King Philip was killed by Benjamin Church's troops. They were led to him by one of Philip's followers who was angry because Philip had just killed his brother for suggesting that they try to make peace with the English. Thus, Philip's heavy-handedness with his own people brought about his final downfall. With Philip's death, the war was pretty much over, though it would take a couple more years before the fighting was finished. And while the English colonists officially "won" the war, it was a war that everyone lost in the end.

A Time Line of Some of the Events Connected with King Philip's War

July 1662
Josiah Winslow forces Alexander, sachem of the Pokanokets, to a meeting in Plymouth. Alexander dies shortly after the meeting, and his brother Philip (also known as Metacom) becomes sachem.

January 1675
Sassamon tells Governor Josiah Winslow that Philip is preparing for war. Soon after this, Sassamon is found dead.

June 1, 1675
Three followers of Philip are put on trial for the murder of Sassamon. Two of them are hanged soon after. The third was taken from jail and killed once the war started.

June 20, 1675
Philip's warriors burn down two houses in Kickemuit, a part of Swansea.

June 23, 1675
The first shot in the war occurs when a boy in Swansea shoots and kills an Indian who was looting some houses.

June 24, 1675
Swansea is attacked and at least ten people are killed, including the boy who fired the first shot in the war.

June-October 1675
Middleborough, Dartmouth, Mendon, Brookfield, Lancaster, Deerfield, Hadley, Northfield, and Springfield are attacked.

December 19, 1675
The Great Swamp Fight

January 1676
The Hungry March

February 1676
Philip loses a major battle with the Mohawks in New York where he had gone to secure more allies and spend the winter.

Winter of 1675/1676
Andover, Bridgewater, Chelmsford, Groton, Marlborough, Medfield, Medford, Millis, Plymouth, Portland, Providence, Scituate, Simsbury, Sudbury, Suffield, Warwick, Weymouth, and Wrentham are attacked.

February 10, 1676
Lancaster is attacked and Mary Rowlandson is captured.

February 1676
The Concord Praying Indians are taken from John Hoar's custody and brought to Deer Island.

March 1676
Captain Pierce and his men are killed, and Rehoboth is attacked soon after.

April 1676
Canonchet, a Narragansett sachem, is killed.

May 1676
Mary Rowlandson is ransomed.

August 1676
King Philip is killed.

Partial Bibliography

Books Written by People Who Lived Through King Philip's War

The Narrative of the Captivity and Restoration of Mrs. Mary Rowlandson
By Mary Rowlandson, first printed in 1682
Available for free online at http://books.google.com

Entertaining Passages Relating to Philip's War
By Benjamin Church, 1716

A Historical Account of the Doings and Sufferings of the Christian Indians of New England
By Daniel Gookin
Printed in "Archaeologia Americana: Transactions and Collections of the American Antiquarian Society," Volume II, 1836

Other Sources

Mayflower
By Nathaniel Philbrick, Penguin Books, 2006

King Philip's War
By Eric B. Schultz and Michael J. Tougias, The Countryman Press, 1999

History of the Town of Lancaster, Massachusetts:
From the First Settlement to the Present Time,
1643-1876
By Rev. Abijah P. Marvin, 1879

A History of the Town of Concord
By Lemuel Shattuck, 1835

Soldiers in King Philip's War
By George Madison Bodge, 1906

The History of Rehoboth,
Bristol County, Massachusetts
By Leonard Bliss, Jr., 1836

The Hoar Family in America
and Its English Ancestry
By Henry Stedman Nourse, 1899

The Whitcomb Family in America:
A Biographical Genealogy
By Charlotte Whitcomb, 1904

Kingsley Genealogy
By Leroy Brown, M.D. 1907

The Naked Quaker
True Crimes and Controversies from the Courts of
Colonial New England
By Diane Rapaport, 2007

Praise for Susan Kilbride's
Science Unit Studies for Homeschoolers and Teachers

If you are looking for quality science units, but simply don't have the time to put a unit together, Susan's book is perfect for you. If you want to supplement your existing science program, I definitely recommend taking a close look at the book. Those of you who might be a little scared of trying to put together your own science lessons for fear you might get something wrong, fear no more....
Jackie from Quaint Scribbles

This collection of fun science lessons and activities are designed to offer hands on experiments that will satisfy the curious nature of children, while making it easier for parents to teach science.
Kathy Davis of HomeschoolBuzz.com

If you're looking for a science unit study homeschool program that is easy to use and is comprehensive and worth using, then you should check out "Science Unit Studies for Homeschoolers and Teachers." I recently read through the book and really liked what I saw.
Heidi Johnson of Homeschool-how-to.com

....the conversational style and logical, easy-to-follow instructions certainly make this a recommended and useful tool for any parent; especially those that may be uncomfortable or unfamiliar with teaching science.
Jeanie Frias of California Homeschooler

You make learning science fun!
Brianna, homeschooler, age 10

I think "Science Unit Studies for Homeschoolers and Teachers" is a good value and provides a lot of fun, hands-on science for homeschoolers.

Courtney Larson, The Old Schoolhouse® Magazine

The wealth of information included therein is amazing and the material is novice friendly. I would definitely recommend "Science Unit Studies for Homeschoolers and Teachers."

Bridgette Taylor with Hearts at Home Curriculum

Susan's book is full of so many activities that one would have a very full study of general science over the course of a school year if every activity were completed. I teach a General Science class at a local homeschool co-op and I am implementing a lot of the activities in this book into my class this year. There are even short quizzes (complete with answer keys) provided for the older student unit studies. The quizzes are multiple choice in format and cover the main points students should glean from each unit. I highly recommend this book for any science teacher or student. It really makes the teaching of science quite simple and fun. Overall I give Susan's book 5+ stars.

Heart of the Matter Online

We used "Science Unit Studies for Homeschoolers and Teachers" at home as part of our homeschooling science lessons. The directions were easy to follow and I loved that they used materials that could be purchased from the grocery store. My children, ages 5, 7, and 9, became excited about learning science, actually jumping up and down when it was time to start science lessons!

Ilya Perry, homeschooling mother of three with a degree in elementary education

53144208R00088

Made in the USA
San Bernardino, CA
07 September 2017